Raffie on the Run

Raffie on the Run

Jacqueline Resnick
Pictures by Joe Sutphin

ROARING BROOK PRESS · NEW YORK

Library of Congress Control Number: 2017944673
ISBN: 978-1-62672-866-0

Our books may be purchased in bulk for promotional, educational, or business use. Please
contact your local bookseller or the Macmillan Corporate and Premium Sales Department
at (800) 221-7945 ext. 5442 or by e-mail at MacmillanSpecialMarkets@macmillan.com.

First edition, 2018
Book design by Elizabeth H. Clark
Printed in the United States of America by LSC Communications, Harrisonburg, Virginia

1   3   5   7   9   10   8   6   4   2

For Florence, with endless love

Contents

Raffie on the Run

Prologue

Every day at 2:28 p.m., Lily Wilson gets a slice of pizza. She doesn't want the pizza. It's the brainchild of her babysitter, Beverly, whose job it is to make sure Lily gets safely from school to the subway station, eight blocks away. "Children need fuel," Beverly likes to say, and Lily can't argue, because Beverly was a professional nanny for forty years and is therefore always right in the eyes of Lily's mom.

"Eat, child," Beverly urges as she walks Lily down the steps of Brooklyn's Bergen Street subway station.

Lily takes a bite and makes a big show of chewing, even though she isn't the least bit hungry. *I'm too old for a babysitter*, she thinks as she waves goodbye to Beverly.

She swipes her subway card and pushes through the steel turnstile onto the platform. Then, like she does every day at 2:34 p.m., she walks to the closest trash can, and she throws out her slice of pizza.

Today, a flash of gray catches her eye as she sits down to wait for the train. It's a tiny gray subway rat scurrying along the platform. She stays still, watching him. He's surprisingly cute, with big, round eyes and a fuzzy snout. He's so small he'd look more like a mouse if it weren't for the long rat's tail swishing behind him.

The low rumble of a train nears the station, and immediately the rat picks up speed. *I wonder where he lives*, Lily thinks. *I wonder if he has a family.* She watches as the little rat squeezes through a hole in the wall.

I bet he does, she decides. *I bet somewhere behind that wall, the rat has a home.*

Rat Race

I scurry along a pipe, the smell of pizza still fresh in my snout. I climb over a cinder block, weave around a glob of dust, and squeeze through a crack in the insulation. I strike a pose as my paws land on the woven straw-wrapper rug in my family's living nook. "Selfie!" I declare. I picked that word up from a human recently. It's a fancy way of announcing your arrival.

"Raffie!" My baby brother, Oggie, jumps off the chair I crafted for him out of a dirt-stuffed sock. He scurries over to me, his whiskers twitching with excitement. "Did you see the pizza? Did you did you did you?"

I laugh as I head over to our new row of cupboards. It took my dad months to forage enough cereal boxes to build them. "Maybe," I tease. "And maybe it's only missing a single bite this time."

"Yum yum yum," Oggie cheers.

Everyone has their favorite food. Dad loves slurping up sour milk. Mom is a fan of day-old curries. My older sister, Lulu, never turns down rotten fruit. But Oggie and I have a shared love. Sour tomato sauce . . . moldy cheese . . . hardened crust . . . There is nothing in the world better than a slice of aged pizza.

I pull a white paper carton out of the cupboard. It's filled with the slop my mom mixes up out of leftover forages. This one smells of blackened bananas and melted ice cream and hardened noodles and just a hint of sticky rice.

I fill two bottle caps and nudge one over to Oggie. "Snack is served."

"I don't want slop," Oggie whines. "I want pizza!" He presses his snout against mine and blinks his big, round eyes. "Pleaaaaase, Raffie?"

"I'll go forage it as soon as Mom or Dad gets back to watch you," I promise. "They'll kill me if they find out I left you alone just to go check for the pizza. Besides, what do I always say?"

Oggie slurps up his slop in a single bite. "Aged pizza is the best pizza," he recites.

"Exactly." I lap up my own slop. "The longer that pizza ages in the treasure chest, the better it will taste."

There's a loud clatter behind us. I turn around to see Lulu pushing her way through an air vent. She's wearing ketchup packets on her paws, a paper sleeve from a cup around her stomach, and colorful twist ties braided up her tail. My sister has a passion for fashion. "No forages?" I ask, eying Lulu's empty paws.

"The thief is early," she tells us. "We're clearing the station."

Oggie's eyes meet mine. "Our pizza," he breathes.

I scurry to the spying hole. I'm still too small to see out of it, so I climb onto my espresso cup stool. On the other side of the subway tracks, I see the thief in his bright yellow vest. He's stomping toward one of the station's treasure chests, carrying the black bag he uses to rob us. My heart thuds wildly. Once he empties that treasure chest, he'll rob the one on our side of the tracks. The one with the slice of pizza in it.

"Thief alert! Thief alert!" I hear my dad before I see him.

He pushes through a crack in some insulation, followed closely by my mom. She's panting as she takes a head count. "Lulu, Raffie, Oggie. Thank the trash you're all here." She collapses on her favorite chair, the one she built out of a tissue box when Oggie was born. "I panic when the thief comes early. You know how much he hates rats. When I think about what happened to your great-uncle Reed . . ." She shudders.

My dad brings her a thimble of lemon sewer water. "But we're all home, safe and sound. Here, drink this, honey."

Oggie squeezes onto the stool next to me. We both peer out into the subway station. On the other side of the tracks, the thief is knotting his black bag of plunders. "You'll save our pizza, right?" Oggie whispers to me.

I scrunch up my snout. "I don't—"

"You can do anything!" Oggie continues. "Just like in your stories. Raffie the Unstoppable! Remember how you stopped a runaway train single-pawed? And chased a wild cat off the platform?"

I look away. "I don't think I—"

"You did!" Oggie beams. "You told me!" He lowers

his voice. "A thief is nothing to Raffie the Unstoppable, right?"

I watch the thief toss the bulging bag onto his shoulder. He's still across the tracks. "Right, um . . . of course." I straighten up tall and try to ignore the trembling in my paws. "You distract Mom and Dad," I whisper. "Raffie the Unstoppable is going to get you that pizza!"

Oggie's tail whips in happy circles as he hops down from the stool. He grabs a foil burrito wrapper out of the cupboard. "Look, Mom! See what I can make!"

Oggie gnaws at the foil until it begins to resemble a rat. My little brother is a very talented gnawer. I wait until everyone is *ooh*ing over Oggie's skills. Then I slip through a hole in the wall and scurry out to the platform.

CHAPTER 2

A Cat-and-Mouse Game

T he treasure chest closest to our home is the best one in the station. It's always overflowing with soggy newspapers and empty cups and food— such good food! Slimy ham! Melted chocolate! Mushy eggs! Stale muffins! Food that has rotted and festered, turned crusty and gooey. Food that has melted in the heat or hardened in the cold. Food that has spoiled, spoiled, spoiled, all day long.

I scamper up to the rounded metal edge of the treasure chest and peer down. There it is: a perfect triangle of pizza, with only one bite missing. The pizza isn't as old and moldy as I'd like, but fresh pizza is better than no pizza.

Warm, stale air rushes into the subway station as, out on the tracks, a train announces its arrival with a shriek. On the other side of the tracks, the thief hauls his loot toward the stairs. He'll arrive on my side of the station any minute, carrying a fresh black bag to rob us with.

I slip into the treasure chest as the doors of the train swish open. The conductor's voice echoes through the station. "This is Bergen Street, Brooklyn. Next stop, Jay Street–MetroTech. Stand clear of the closing doors, please." Humans pour off the train, scattering left and right, filling the station with their voices. But I'm far enough inside the treasure chest that none of them spot me. The smell of pizza fills my snout. Oggie is going to be one happy baby.

"That pizza's mine."

I whip around to find Ace Kellogg clambering into the treasure chest.

My fur stands on end. Ace is one of the biggest, strongest, fastest rats in the station. He can outrun the tallest of humans; he can dislodge the heaviest of forages; he can leap over the tracks' electric third rail without ruffling a single strand of fur.

And he never lets anyone forget it.

"Did you really think a *mouse* could score a forage like that?" Ace sneers.

"I am not a mouse," I say through gritted incisors.

The station empties out as the train roars its goodbye. Soon, there's just a single set of footsteps moving down the stairs. I'd recognize those footsteps anywhere. They belong to the thief. We don't have long.

Ace's eyes meet mine. His whiskers twitch greedily. "Okay then, may the best rat eat!"

I lift my tail and dive for the pizza. My paws splay out. My whiskers fly back. I'm going to get this—

Ace crashes into me from the side. I go tumbling away from the pizza. "AHHH!" I smack into the side of the treasure chest. I claw at the metal wall, but I can't get a grip.

"Ow!" I land headfirst inside a paper carton of pea-nutty noodles. On the other side of the carton, I can hear Ace laughing.

I flip myself right side up and paw a noodle off my

eye. Ace is standing on top of the slice of pizza, cheese dripping down his snout. Outside the treasure chest, I hear the thief's footsteps reach the bottom of the stairs. "Oh, did I bump into you, Mouse?" Ace sneers. "You're so small I didn't even see you there."

"I. Am. Not. A. Mouse," I hiss. "I am Raffie the Unstoppable! And that pizza is mine." I leap out of the carton. But my paw gets tangled in a noodle and my tail is stuck in some sticky sauce. Instead of flying fiercely toward Ace, I go tumbling into a cup of water.

I come out sopping wet.

Ace is laughing hysterically as he lifts the pizza in his teeth. I surge toward him. I grab the crust in my incisors and yank with all my might. The pizza doesn't budge from his grip. "You wish," Ace says through a mouthful of cheese. With the pizza gripped firmly in his teeth, he scampers up the side of the treasure chest. He pauses on the rim. "Poor itty-bitty Raffie." He tears off a tiny piece of crust and tosses it down to me. "Here. You can have my scraps, Mouse."

With a snort, he disappears, taking the pizza with him. I'm shaking with fury as I lift the scrap of crust in my teeth. That pizza should have been mine! I spotted it first! I can already imagine the disappointment on Oggie's face when I come home empty-pawed.

The creak of a turnstile makes me jump. The thief is close. I need to get out of here. I crawl out of the treasure chest, slipping a little on my wet paws, and skitter as fast as I can into a shadow.

"RAT!"

I spin around.

The thief is in the middle of the platform. His eyes meet mine. I've been spotted.

"No, no, no, no, no," the thief says. "Nonononono." His voice is low and piercing. He's doing his battle cry.

A shiver starts in my tail and runs all the way up to my ears. Great-Uncle Reed heard a battle cry once, and he never came home. My limbs feel heavier than a bottle full of soda. *Run*, I tell myself. But I can't move; I can hardly even breathe.

The thief's eyes are glued to mine. "Nonononono," he keeps saying. He takes several slow and deliberate steps backward. He's doing his battle dance.

My heart is galloping in my chest and I'm shaking all over, but still my paws won't budge. I get a bad taste in my mouth, like I accidentally ate a bag of vegetables before they rotted. *This is it*, I think. *I'm going to end up just like Great-Uncle Reed.*

The sound of a bell shakes me out of my stupor. It's my family alarm. They're telling me to get home.

I think of Oggie, waiting worriedly for my return. "I'm coming, little brother," I whisper. My eyes find a nearby air vent that leads to home. This time, when I yank at my paws, they lift. I run faster than I ever have in my life. Past the tall green beam painted with classi-fied human codes. Over a wad of doughnut mashed into the platform crack. I'm breathing hard by the time I reach the air vent. The thief is still saying his battle cry as I dive headfirst through it.

I land in a heap in our living room. My mom is franti-cally sounding our alarm. Oggie bounds over and nuz-zles against me. "What happened?" he gasps. "Tell me everything!"

"I—" I begin.

"I don't want to hear it," my mom cuts in. "Do you know how dangerous that was, Raffie? We heard the thief's battle cry!"

"What were you thinking?" my dad continues. "You know the rules, Raffie."

"I—" I begin again, but this time, my dad cuts me off. "You *do* know the rules, right?" He wrings his tail be-tween his front paws. "What's the first rule of rathood?"

I study the straw-wrapper rug at my paws. "Never be spotted."

"Yes! Never be spotted!" my mom explodes. "Espe-cially by the thief!"

"And what's the second rule of rathood?" my dad presses.

"Never cross the tracks without a parent," I mutter.

"That's right," my dad says. "Now, tell me what the final rule of rathood is."

"Never set paw in the Roadway," I recite.

"Ever," my dad adds darkly.

I can't help but shiver. Every subway rat knows about the Roadway. It's an underground pathway through the city, a dark, sinister place, made up of sewers and pipes and abandoned subway tunnels. Only the most soulless of rats live down there, rats who would strike out against one another just to survive. And there are snakes too, and evil cats, and—a shudder runs through me—rattraps and rat poison, everywhere.

Oggie scoots closer to me. I wind my tail through his. "It's okay, Oggie," my mom says. She gives him a nuzzle. "As long as you follow the rules of rathood, you'll be fine. Which means no more run-ins with the thief." She gives me a pointed look. "Got it?"

My whiskers droop. "Got it," I mumble.

"Good." My dad lets out a sigh. "It's for your own safety, Raffie. Remember that. Now, off to your room. Your mom and I will decide your punishment."

I slink off to the bedroom I share with Oggie and Lulu. Oggie rushes in after me. "Where's the pizza?" he whispers. "Did you get it? Did you hide it somewhere safe? Did you did you?"

The tiny piece of crust is still tucked away in the back of my mouth. I spit it onto the ground. "I brought you crust," I tell him.

Oggie's whiskers quiver. Disappointment floods his face. "Where's sauce? Where's cheese?"

I look down. "I . . . uh . . ."

"Did the thief battle you?" Oggie gasps.

I fidget from paw to paw. "Well . . . um . . ."

"Was it a scary battle?" Oggie asks eagerly. "Was it dangerous? It was, wasn't it?"

I look up. Oggie's eyes are wide with excitement. "Yes," I say slowly. "Yes, Oggie, it was." I pace through the room, past the shoe box I sleep in, past the pickle jar Oggie sleeps in and the pink, ribbony shoe Lulu sleeps in, all the way to the matchboxes that hold some of Lulu's accessories. The story is growing in my brain, molding and twisting until I can see it so clearly, I nearly believe it.

"I made it safely into the treasure chest," I tell Oggie. "I had the pizza gripped in my teeth! But then the thief arrived." I let my voice dip lower, so Oggie has to move close to hear me. "Have you ever seen the thief's hand up close, Oggie? It's huge—bigger than Dad's whole body! And that hand reached into the treasure chest . . . right toward me. The thief let out his battle cry, but I refused to back down. You know why, Oggie? Because when it comes to pizza, I have a motto: never give up!"

"Yeah!" Oggie bounces on his paws. "Never give up!"

"That's right. So I held tightly to that pizza and

scurried up the side of the treasure chest. But the thief wouldn't let me go that easily. He grabbed for me! I jumped out of the way just in time, but he got my pizza—which he ripped right out of my mouth. I sacrificed that pizza for my life, Oggie. But I was able to hold on to this one small piece of crust, just for you."

"Wow, Raffie," Oggie breathes. "You really are unstoppable."

I look away, suddenly unable to meet his eyes. I study the station crests that hang on our wall: a Lipton tea bag for my family, a Kellogg cereal label for Ace's family, and a 100% Cashmere tag for the Cashmere family. "Yes," I say. "I really am."

CHAPTER 3

Pack Rats

"P lastic." My mom rolls an empty water bottle over to Lulu.

"Metal." I hand my dad a paper clip. He tosses me a balled-up receipt in return.

We're in the sorting nook, and Oggie and I are on paper duty. Oggie grabs the receipt out of my paws and places it on the stack of napkins and MetroCards and straw wrappers and paper bags and newspapers and envelopes and empty food boxes that my family has foraged over the past week. "Sorting day is the best," he says. "I love being a back rat!"

"*Pack* rat," I correct. I taught him that recently, after I heard a human say it on the platform. The platform is the best place to collect new words and sayings.

"*Pack* rat," Oggie repeats. He curls his tail happily. "Raffie's a great teacher," he informs my family.

"So we've heard." Lulu rolls her eyes. She must have gotten glitter in them again. Lulu likes glitter almost as much as Oggie and I like pizza.

My eyes wander over to the clock. When the toothpick hits lint, Pizza Girl will arrive at the station. She has perfect timing: she gives me just enough time to forage her pizza before rush hour, when we go to bed. Mom and Dad like us to sleep while the station is busiest so we can spend the nighttime hours foraging.

"Ooh, look at this." Lulu dangles something gold and glittery in front of my snout.

"Shiny!" Oggie says.

"It's a yearing, right?" Lulu asks.

"An earring," my dad corrects.

"A dangle earring, to be precise," my mom adds.

My parents know the human names and uses of almost every item. I guess that's what happens when you're older than the hardened wad of gum stuck to the MetroCard machine.

"Dangle earrings are very important," my dad explains. "Humans store them in tiny holes in their ears so they always have a small sword at the ready."

"Wow," Lulu breathes. "Maybe I should wear one—"

"Don't even think about it," my mom warns. "There will be no holes in any ears in this household."

Lulu huffs as she throws the earring into the metal pile. "Here," my mom says. She grabs a shiny sheet of paper off the pile I sorted. "Wear one of these instead." She peels a small white square off the paper. It says *I* ♥ *NY* on it. "It's called a sticker. Humans use them to repair things like notebooks and bags."

Lulu takes the sticker and presses it to Oggie's ear. "Hey!" Oggie cries. "My ear's not broken!" He tries to paw the sticker off, but it's stuck to his fur.

"Hmm." Lulu circles Oggie, studying his ear. Today she's wearing a yellow zipper around her stomach, a white bottle cap on her head, and a glittery pink shoelace knotted up her tail. "It does make Oggie look quite suave . . ." She takes the sheet of stickers from my mom and tosses it into her personal accessories pile. "Thanks!"

"I don't look like a *squab*," Oggie says angrily. He frantically paws at his ear, but the sticker isn't going anywhere.

"Lulu's right," I tell Oggie. "It suits you. It makes you look . . . unstoppable."

Oggie's head snaps up. "Unstoppable? Like you?" I nod, and Oggie bounces excitedly on his paws. "Oggie the Unstoppable!"

Lulu giggles into her paws. "Aren't you getting a little old for those ridiculous stories, Raffie?"

"They're not just stories," Oggie informs her. "Raffie is a hero!"

I straighten up onto my hind legs and puff out my

chest. "That's right," I say. Lulu is still giggling when the clock strikes lint. "I'm going to the kitchen," I announce. "Raffie the Unstoppable needs a snack."

"Bring me an apple core from the cupboard," Lulu says.

"Just the cupboard!" my mom calls after me. "Remember your punishment—"

"No foraging alone," I call back. "I know, I know!"

I head toward the kitchen, but as soon as I'm sure no one's followed me, I make a sharp turn toward the spying hole. I climb onto my espresso cup stool and peer out into the station.

It only takes me a second to spot her.

Pizza Girl.

As usual, she's walking across the platform carrying

a slice of pizza. The smell drifts toward me, sweet and tangy, oozing deliciousness. My snout waters.

"Is there pizza?" At the sound of Oggie's voice, I pull back from the spying hole. Oggie blinks his big, round eyes up at me. The *I ♥ NY* sticker flashes on his ear.

"Pizza Girl brought a slice," I tell him.

Oggie's whiskers twitch in excitement. "Can I look?"

I scoot over and Oggie climbs onto the stool. His snout presses against mine as we peer out at the pizza. "Looks scrumptious," I say.

"Scrumpy," Oggie agrees. He turns to me. "Go get it, Raffie! Please please please?"

I sigh. "You heard Mom. I'm not allowed to forage alone. Besides, what would I do? Just grab it right out of her hands?"

"Yeah!" Oggie nudges me with his snout. "She's not the thief! She looks nice! She never eats it anyway."

I imagine walking up to Pizza Girl and snatching the slice away from her. There would be battle cries. Battle dances. Or worse. I shudder. "No way," I tell Oggie. "A human is a human. And humans can never be trusted."

I watch as Pizza Girl walks over to the treasure chest and tosses the slice. It lands on the edge, the crust dangling off the rim. "Perfect," I say. "It's right on the edge. It will be easy to get when I forage with Dad later."

"Promise?" Oggie begs. "Because I have an idea!

We can let it age at home, and it can be my birthday present!"

Oggie's birthday is in three days, but he's been talking about it for weeks. "Sure," I say.

"Yeah yeah yeah!" Oggie cheers. "Pizza to go with my story!"

Every year for Oggie's birthday, I make up a special Raffie the Unstoppable story just for him. I already have this year's all made up. "Pizza and a story," I agree with a laugh.

A train roars into the station and opens its doors. Two boys climb off. One's carrying a ball. "Go long," he shouts. He throws the ball. It zooms through the air, across the platform.

His friend runs to get it. "They're playing Tail Ball?" Oggie asks. Tail Ball is a game I invented when our station was closed for construction and we were stuck behind the wall for a week straight. I gnawed a pompom off a wool hat and taught Oggie to use his tail to whip it into a soda can. Oggie and I are undefeated in Tail Ball. We beat Lulu, Mom, and Dad every time, even though it's three against two.

"Something like that . . ." I trail off. "Uh-oh," I whisper.

The ball whizzes past the friend—and crashes right into the treasure chest.

The pizza teeters.

It totters.

It slides over the edge of the treasure chest and tumbles to the floor.

"My birthday pizza!" Oggie cries. "We need to get it before something happens to it!"

I look around. The platform is clearing out. A final, lingering man disappears up the stairs. There's not a human in sight. Still, I hesitate. I'm in major trouble after yesterday's run-in with the thief.

"Raffie the Unstoppable will save my pizza," Oggie says. "Right?"

I picture Ace: cheese from the pizza dripping down his snout. *You can have my scraps, Mouse.*

My fur bristles. I stand up tall. "Right," I declare. "You know what I always say when it comes to pizza . . ."

"Never give up!" Oggie cheers.

"Never give up," I repeat. I take a deep breath and squeeze through the spying hole. I'm halfway through when I hear a cough from behind.

I halt.

I know that cough.

"Raffie Lipton! Where do you think you're going?"

I yank myself out of the hole to find my mom glaring down at me.

"I . . . um . . . there were no apple cores in the cupboard, so I was just going to, um, forage one for Lulu," I say.

"Even though we explicitly told you not to?" my mom

explodes. "I can't believe you, Raffie! If the thief spots you again, you know what could happen!"

"The E word, I know. But the platform's empty—"

"Yes, the E word!" my mom interrupts. "With his traps and poison and—I can't even think about it." Her whiskers quiver. "That's it. I'm sending you to bed early tonight. And you too, Oggie." My mom shakes her head. "Think what kind of example you're setting for your little brother, Raffie."

Oggie looks up at me as we file to our bedroom. His eyes are wide with worry. "What about my birthday pizza?"

I flinch at the thought of losing yet another slice of pizza for Oggie. "Don't worry," I whisper. "I'll just have to sneak out when Mom isn't looking."

"Never give up," Oggie whispers back.

I give Oggie a quick nuzzle. "Never give up," I agree.

"To bed, both of you!" our mom says.

CHAPTER

A Sitting Duck

A feast has been abandoned on the other side of the tracks. There are rotten fish heads and moldy sandwiches and half-eaten burritos and pools of chocolate and—yes! Two whole slices of untouched, perfectly aged pizza.

And I'm going to get them.

"You wish, Mouse." Ace appears next to me. He's grown since the last time I saw him, and he towers over me, quadruple my size. "May the best rat eat," he leers.

There's no time to scurry across the tracks if I want to beat Ace. I have to jump.

Ace and I take the leap at the same time. I soar into the air. I'm light as a feather! I'm buoyant as a balloon! I'm—

Creeeeak.

I wake with a start. Adrenaline is pumping through my veins, and it takes me a second to realize that I'm in my shoe box, tucked comfortably beneath my double-ply tissue.

I yawn. It's evening rush hour. Trains are rushing through the station, one after another, making the floor shake soothingly. Faint voices and footsteps float in the distance, the usual lullaby of rush hour, and I feel my eyes drifting shut again.

Creeeeak.

My eyes pop back open. There's that noise again.

I shake off my tissue and sit up. It hits me suddenly that I was supposed to sneak out to forage the slice of pizza for Oggie's birthday present. I must have fallen asleep before I could. I yawn. A thin beam of light streams in from the station, casting a glow over our bedroom. Lulu is tucked inside her pink shoe, wrapped snugly in its silky ribbons. She lets out a soft snore. I look over at Oggie's pickle jar. Behind the McClure's label, I see a soft layer of pencil shavings and—nothing else.

Oggie is not in his bed.

I suddenly feel like I've eaten one too many rotten potatoes.

Oggie is *never* not in his bed. Every night, he gets into bed right before me, and when it's time to get up, I'm the one to wake him.

I hop down from my shoe box and scurry out of our room. "Oggie?" I whisper. "Where are you?" I check the kitchen and the living nook and the dining nook, but there's no tiny gray snout poking into the cupboards and no tiny gray paws curled up in the tissue box chair, and no tiny gray rat slurping leftovers off the dining table Dad built out of four nails and a cardboard box.

"Oggie?" I try again. "Stop playing. You're scaring me." I peek into the sorting nook. It's empty except for the neatly sorted piles of paper, metal, plastic, gadgets, and Lulu's accessories. There's only one place left to look.

I tiptoe into Mom and Dad's room. They're sprawled out in their Tupperware container, fast asleep. Their paws are entwined, and there's no tiny third set mixed in with them. I'm not surprised. Oggie never climbs into their bed when he's scared; he always climbs into mine.

I sneak out of their room. "Oggie," I whisper. "Come here right now." I turn in a circle, waiting. Oggie didn't just vanish into thin air. He has to be here *somewhere*.

Unless . . .

No.

He wouldn't.

I sprint to the spying hole and climb onto my stool. Out in the station, the platform is packed with humans. There are humans in suits and humans in dresses, humans carrying bags and humans gripping phones, tiny humans and enormous humans, humans laughing and humans scowling, one after another after another, so many humans they blend into a single mass of hair and faces and arms and legs.

My eyes drop to the floor. It's a traffic jam of feet. I scan from sneaker to sandal to heel. Finally my eyes land on the strip of dark green tile that runs along the bottom of the wall. Pressed against the tile, creeping slowly forward, is Oggie, the *I ♥ NY* sticker still pasted to his ear.

"No," I gasp. I thrust my snout through the spying hole. Oggie is camouflaged enough by the tiles that so

far no humans have noticed him. I have to get him to come home before one does.

"Oggie!" I hiss. "Come back this instant!" I sound exactly like Mom, but I don't care. "I'm serious, Oggie! Get in here!" But trains are racing into the station on both sides of the tracks, and Oggie doesn't hear me. He keeps creeping forward, his eyes focused on something in the distance.

I follow his gaze.

There, being sidestepped by dozens of humans, is the slice of pizza that was knocked out of the treasure chest earlier. The one I was supposed to forage for him.

A train stops on the tracks, panting like a rat out of breath. Humans jostle and patter, pouring off the train and cramming themselves on. With a sputter, the train lurches down the tracks again, vanishing into the blackness of the tunnels.

I squeeze through the hole. I don't care how many rules I'm about to break. I have to help Oggie. I race out to the platform and press myself against the wall.

Through the rumble of footsteps, I catch a snippet of his voice. "Never give up! Oggie the Unstoppable! Just like Raffie!"

A dark, sticky feeling spreads through my stomach. "No, Oggie!" I shout. But another train roars into the station, rattling my bones and swallowing up my voice.

My brother weaves through the maze of human feet, going straight for the pizza.

"Rat!" someone screams.

Suddenly the station is filled with battle cries.

"Eeeeek!"

"Gross!"

"Ew!"

People jump and shove toward the exit. I leap out of the way of a high heel. It hits the ground with a sickening crunch, right where I stood only seconds before. I flatten myself against the wall, trembling all over. "Oggie! Stop!" I shout. But Oggie's already halfway down the platform. He doesn't hear me.

"I see one! I actually see one, Tess!" The voice belongs to a boy. He's pushing his way through the crowded platform. A girl follows behind him. "I can't believe there's finally a rat on the platform instead of the tracks. I've been looking for weeks!"

Tess wrinkles her nose. "Yeah, and it's been disgusting for weeks, Tyler."

My heart seizes. They're walking straight toward Oggie.

Tyler drops his backpack and kneels down near Oggie. "Look at him, Tess. He's even got an *I ♥NY* sticker on his ear. He's perfect."

I wait for Oggie to run. But he stands frozen in place. He's shaking all over, his eyes locked on the pizza.

· 32 ·

"What are you doing, Oggie?" I shout. "Come home this instant!"

I'm itching to run to him, but one rat on the platform is bad enough. If humans see two . . . I shudder. The E word will be here faster than I can say *rat poison*. I stay pressed against the wall. "Oggie!" I try again.

Oggie's snout snaps up. Across the platform, his eyes meet mine. *Finally.* My whiskers droop with relief. "Come here," I mouth.

Oggie's eyes dart between the pizza and me. He doesn't move.

"Perfect is not the word I'd use," Tess says as I wave my tail frantically at Oggie. "Will you just forget this already, Tyler?"

"No way," Tyler says. "I'm going to bring a subway rat to school for our class pet competition if it's the last thing I do. It will be the best fifth-grade prank of all time!" Tyler pulls something out of his backpack and drops it on the ground. My heart splinters faster than a glass bottle on the tracks.

It's a cage.

"OGGIE!" I shout.

I don't care about being spotted anymore. I have to get to Oggie. I have to save him. I give up the protection of the wall and dash down the platform.

"Come, little rat," Tyler sings. "Go in the box."

Tess rolls her eyes. "It's never happening, Tyler. You

don't just *catch* a subway rat. Here, you really want to catch something?" She kicks the slice of pizza. It goes skidding into the cage. "There. You caught some pizza! Congratulations. Now can we please go—"

"Tess." Tyler grabs her arm. "Look." They both watch as Oggie inches slowly toward the cage. "I think he wants the pizza," Tyler breathes.

I race toward Oggie. "Stop!" I scream. "It's a trap!" But another train rushes into the station, drowning out my voice.

People spill off the train. I dodge feet left and right. "Don't do it, Oggie!" I yell, but the footsteps stomp out my voice. I catch a glimpse of Oggie through a pair of legs. He steps into the cage.

"No!" I howl as the door of the cage slams shut behind him.

"Got him!" I hear Tyler say. "I can't believe it. I actually caught one!"

I shove between a pair of yellow heels and leap over a brown shoe. "Rat!" someone shrieks. More battle cries follow, but I barely notice.

"I'm coming, Oggie!" I shout.

The train conductor's voice echoes through the station. "Next stop, Jay Street–MetroTech."

Tyler slips a cover over Oggie's cage. "There." He grins. "Now he can't cause any trouble."

Tess shakes her head. "Come on, rat boy. Mrs. Horowitz will kill us if we're late for tonight's play rehearsal." She grabs Tyler's arm and pulls him onto the train. I make it to the edge of the platform just as the doors of the train click shut.

Through the window, I see the cage rattling in Tyler's arms.

"Oggie!" I scream.

The train kicks to a start and zooms out of the station, taking Oggie with it.

CHAPTER 5

Fly the Coop

"Oggie!" I gallop down the platform after the train. This can't be happening. This can't be real.

I skid to a stop at the end of the platform, where the tracks leave the station. I catch a glimpse of the back of the train, and then it melts into the blackness of the tunnels, and all that's left is silence.

"Oggie," I sob.

He's gone.

My little brother is gone.

And it's all my fault.

I think of him saying, "Oggie the Unstoppable! Just like Raffie!" If I hadn't told him all those stories . . . made him believe I was unstoppable . . . when really . . .

My throat closes up and I gasp for air.

I slump to the ground and bury my snout in my paws. I hear the vague sounds of battle cries in the distance,

but I don't care. Let them battle me. Let them chase me. Oggie's gone. Nothing matters anymore.

A train rumbles into the station on the other side of the tracks. The air is a tunnel of noise as the doors open and the conductor shouts and people shove on and off. I steal a glance at the wall that leads to home. Behind that wall, Mom, Dad, and Lulu are sleeping peacefully, unaware that with every passing second, Oggie is getting farther and farther away.

A sob racks through me. How am I ever going to tell them?

I look away, and something catches my eye next to the treasure chest. A backpack.

My chest squeezes.

It's Tyler's backpack. The boy who took Oggie.

I leap to my paws. Maybe there's something in there that can help me find my brother! I gallop toward the backpack, dodging shoes left and right. Blood pounds in my ears. All I can hear is Oggie's voice, stuck on repeat in my head. *Just like Raffie. Just like Raffie.*

The backpack is crumpled in a heap on the floor. The zipper is partially open. I slip through the opening and crawl inside. Immediately I smell food. I take a quick sniff. An apple, a juice, and an oatmeal-raisin cookie. I push past the food, uninterested. For the first time in my life, I'm not hungry.

I nose my way past two books, three coins, a white ball, four clumps of lint, a dust bunny, six empty candy wrappers, and one of those sharp, inky weapons humans use to write. I'm panting when I stop in front of a small notebook. I climb on top of it. Underneath my paws is a string of letters.

I'm not the best reader, but I squint, concentrating hard. "Centaur—center—no, Central," I whisper. "Parl—no, Park—"

A sudden jolt sends me reeling backward. The backpack is being lifted in the air. I'm slammed into the side, the breath knocked out of me.

"Looks like some kid lost a backpack," I hear a muffled voice say. The bag swings through the air, sending me tumbling toward the gap in zipper.

"No," I gasp. I sink my teeth into the fabric just in time. Only my tail flies out of the bag. I yank it back inside, breathing hard.

"I'm going to bring it to the ticket booth," I hear the voice say.

"If you see something, say something," another voice replies jokingly.

The contents of the bag toss wildly around. I duck out of the way of the ball and claw back to the notebook. A coin slams into my back, sending pain shooting down my paws. Beneath me, letters swim in front of my eyes.

Focus, I order myself.

Slowly, words begin to take shape.

Central Park Day School

220 Central Park West, Class 5B

The bag swings again, sending the ball smacking into me. I yelp in pain. Through the opening in the zipper, I catch a glimpse of the turnstiles. After the turnstiles comes the ticket booth and Marcus the teller. Marcus who has "no patience for rats, I tellya!" I've heard him say it many, many times.

There's a whoosh of air from behind as a train nears the station. I think of what Tyler said. He's bringing Oggie to school like some kind of pet.

Pieces click together in my mind, one after another.

Central Park Day School

220 Central Park West, Class 5B

It's the location of the school where Tyler is bringing Oggie! It has to be.

I need to get out of this bag. The backpack bumps against the metal turnstiles, sending me somersaulting backward. I scramble to my paws. Outside, I see the turnstile swinging past. I only have a second before we reach the ticket booth.

I squeeze through the gap in the zipper and leap onto one of the turnstiles. "Oh my goodness!" someone shouts. "Did a rat just come out of that bag?"

I don't wait to hear the response. I scurry down from the turnstile. My paws are shaking and my heart is pounding and all I can think is *220 Central Park West.*

A train screeches to a stop on the tracks. It's the train that goes into the city. The same one that Tyler and Tess took with Oggie. "Next stop, Jay Street–MetroTech," the conductor announces. "Stand clear of the closing doors, please."

I race under the turnstiles and across the platform. The train looms in front of me, jam-packed with humans. I'm shaking so hard I can barely feel my paws.

220 Central Park West.

I have to get there. I have to get to Oggie.

I squeeze between a pair of legs and jump onto the train. The doors swish shut behind me.

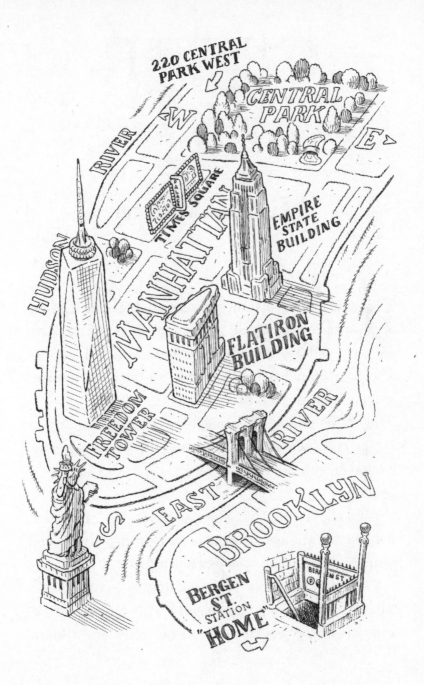

CHAPTER

6

A Fish out of Water

Panic hits me instantly. There are feet and legs and arms and hands all around me. So many humans, packed together like noodles in a carton. I dodge a heel and crouch behind an ankle. My tail hits a sneaker and I quickly draw it back.

My heart pounds. The enemy is everywhere.

The train seems to spin around me: feet, wall, feet, wall, feet, cup, fee—

Cup!

It's a paper cup, laying on its side on the train floor. It's just big enough to fit a rat. I hold my breath and scurry toward it. *No one look down,* I beg silently.

I leap into the cup. I'm trembling as I curl up in a ball. My head bumps against the stiff paper bottom, and something wet drops onto my whiskers. I know that smell. It's the powerful potion humans use to get their morning jolt. I quickly lick it up. A fizzy feeling spreads through me. I suddenly feel like I could scurry around the subway station a hundred times. "I can do this," I whisper to myself. I just need to get under one of the train's benches to hide.

"So much litter," a man grumbles nearby. I hear a foot stomp next to me. I peek out the open end of the cup. A shiny black shoe lifts in the air. It swings. It knocks into my cup.

I paw desperately, but there's nothing I can do—my cup goes rolling across the floor.

I spin round and round. My stomach roils. My vision blurs. The cup skids over something slippery and rolls even faster.

"Mommy, that cup has a tail!"

My heart seizes. I grab my tail and yank it back inside the cup.

"Shhh, honey," a woman says. "You're disturbing the other passengers."

I roll faster. Up becomes down and down becomes up. My last meal of slop rises in my throat. I'm about to be sick when I suddenly crash to a stop.

I peek shakily out of the cup. I see a glass bottle. A wad of napkins. A shiny silver wall. But no feet. Slowly, it hits me: I've rolled underneath a bench.

My stomach settles down. I take a deep breath. I'm okay. No one can see me down here. I have time to come up with a plan.

I close my eyes and think. *How do I find Oggie?*

No answers come.

I think harder.

I could . . .

Or maybe . . .

What about . . .

No, no, no.

The tracks clatter beneath the train, sending vibrations through my paws. The conductor's voice spills through the car: "This is Jay Street–MetroTech . . ."

Footsteps shake like thunder. The conductor's voice booms. "Next stop, York Street."

What was I *thinking* getting on this train? I have no clue how to get to 220 Central Park West. What if that's not even where Tyler was taking Oggie? What if this train goes somewhere different? What if it goes to . . . the E word?

A tremble runs through me. My parents won't say such a bad word out loud, but I've heard it anyway. *Exterminator.*

I shake harder. What if I just boarded a train to the exterminator?

"Okay, don't panic," I whisper to myself. I'm safe under this bench. I'll just ride the train until I figure out what to do. There's no reason to be scared.

SCREECH!

A horrible, piercing sound fills the air as the train jerks to a short stop. I'm tossed out of my cup. I extract my claws, but I'm not fast enough. I go sliding out from under the bench for everyone to see.

I skid across the train on my belly. My tail whips against a pole. My whiskers brush a shoe. I slam to a stop against a high heel. A squeak of terror escapes me.

"It's—it's—" a woman sputters. "RAT!"

I've been spotted.

Battle cries erupt on every side of me. Legs move

frantically: pushing and running and jumping on top of benches. "Get it out of here!" someone screams.

A can smashes into my tail. I cry out in pain.

The train doors slide open. "This is York Street," the conductor announces.

A man leans toward me. He has a rolled-up newspaper in his hand. "Get away," he growls. He swats me with the newspaper. *Hard.*

I'm lifted into the air.

"Ahhh!" I scream. My whiskers tangle. My ears flap. I tumble through the open train door.

The train erupts with cheers as I crash down on the subway station platform.

I drag myself to my paws. I wobble a little as I push through a crowd of feet. Shrieks fill the air. "It touched my foot!" someone yells. I have to get away.

I scurry as fast as my wobbly legs will carry me. This station is enormous. I race around pillar after pillar. Past a booth with a man in it. Up two flights of stairs and down a long tunnel. Everytime I slow down, I hear another battle cry. I keep going. I have to get somewhere safe.

I race up a stairwell. My paws feel as bendy as straws as I burst through a doorway. I collapse behind a round, black treasure chest. I want to think I've found a safe spot, but strange noises meet my ears. A honk. A zoom. A beep.

Cars.

My chest squeezes. Slowly, I peek around the treasure chest. A yellow car whizzes past. A biker pedals behind it. I look up. There's no ceiling, no rafters. There's just sky. It burns brightly, the color of an orange peel before it rots. A breeze blows past, carrying on it strangely fresh smells.

My fur stands straight up.

I'm not underground anymore.

CHAPTER 7

Birds of a Feather Flock Together

"220 Central Park West. 220 Central Park West." I mutter the address to myself as I scurry down the street. New smells swirl around me. Asphalt and car fumes and leaves and dirt and food that's all wrong: fresh instead of rotten, savory instead of stale, sweet instead of sour. The smells slide down my throat, turning my stomach.

I hear a gasp from up above, and I dart behind a bush, out of sight. I've only been aboveground twice before. Both times I was with my dad, and we stayed near our station. Even still, my dad drove me crazy with safety questions for days beforehand.

"What do you do if you run into a human?" my dad asked for the eight thousandth time.

"The three Ds, Dad. I know!"

"And the three Ds are?" my dad pressed.

"Duck, dash, disappear. I got it. Let's go already!"

"Yeah, we got it!" Oggie agreed. He was racing in circles around us. "Let's go go go!"

"You aren't going anywhere, Oggie," my dad said. "You're too young. You'll have your sidewalk survival lesson when you're Raffie's age."

"No fair!" Oggie pouted, but my dad wouldn't change his mind.

"There's a lot you don't know about the world above," my dad told us. "There are unimaginable dangers up there."

"Worse than thieves?" Oggie gasped.

"Much," my dad said gravely. "Aboveground is no place for a baby."

Those words echo in my head now as I crouch behind the bush. I have to get to Oggie.

I dash into a shadow on the sidewalk. There's no way I can get back on that train. I'll have to find another way to Oggie. A sparrow hops past me. "Excuse me," I call out. "Do you know how to get to 220 Central Park West?"

"Park West!" the sparrow squeaks. "Southwest! I'm a compass!" She collapses in a fit of giggles. I scurry past her and chase after a squirrel.

"Hello!" I call out. "Do you know how to get to 220 Central Park West?" The squirrel snatches something off the ground and scampers silently up a tree.

I look around. Cars crawl down the packed street. People jostle along the sidewalks. Buildings stand tall overhead, one stacked next to another. I turn in a circle. I'd forgotten how much *space* there is aboveground. It stretches onward and outward and upward, on and on, for as far as my eyes can see. Down in the subway, wherever you scurry, you'll eventually hit a wall. Up here, there are no walls.

I look above me, and my breath catches in my throat. High up, in the middle of the sky, there's a road filled with cars. It's wide and it's blue and it's just floating in midair.

Panic twists my stomach into knots. Where *am* I?

"So many rats in this city." A woman's voice drifts down to me.

"About two million," a man replies. "Can you believe that?"

My heart leaps into my throat. That woman saw me. I have to be more careful. "The three Ds," I whisper to myself.

I duck behind a street sign, then dash along the street, careful to disappear into shadows or behind trees.

The sky is getting darker, streaked with black. Lights flicker in the windows. My panic is growing, spilling into my paws and my chest, until even my whiskers quiver with it. Night is falling, and Oggie is out there somewhere, trapped and alone.

I scurry down one street and then another. I have no idea where I'm going, but I can't just stand still. Birds flit through the sky above, touching down on branches and windows. I try to call out to them, but they're never still for long. I spot an oily black bird perched on a bush. "Excuse me," I call up. "Can you tell me where 220 Central Park—"

The bird's gone, swooping away before I can finish my question.

"Hey! Little rat!"

I spin around. The voice belongs to a curly-haired boy. He gallops toward me, holding half a sandwich. "Do you want the rest?" He waves the sandwich at me.

"I don't like it," the boy continues. "Too much cheese! I don't like cheese. It hurts my belly. But rats like cheese, right? Here!" He tosses the sandwich at my paws. I breathe in its scent. My stomach grumbles. Cheese smells good all the time, even when it's fresh.

My eyes dart up to the boy. He smiles at me. He's missing a front tooth. I look back at the sandwich. My stomach grumbles more. It's been a long time since my last meal of slop. "Eat it!" the boy says. "Then I won't have to."

The smell of cheesy goodness draws me closer. Cheese oozes over the sides of the bread, all gooey and melty . . .

No!

I stop short. What am I thinking? I glance at the boy. He's still smiling, watching me.

It's a trick. Or a trap. It has to be. Why else would the boy be smiling?

"Kellan!" A woman runs over, her dark hair flying into her face. "What did I say about wandering away from me? What are you even doing over here . . ." The woman trails off. I feel the heat of her gaze as it lands on me. "Rat," she whispers.

A trap. I knew it.

I abandon the sandwich and scurry away. "Wait!" the boy calls after me. "You forgot my sandwich!"

I scurry faster. There's an enormous green box at the

end of the road. Rotten scents waft out of it. My whiskers twitch. It smells like home. I dive behind it to hide and bump snout-first into something soft and black.

My first thought is *cat*. You never know where you'll find one aboveground. I jump backward, my heart pounding. "Please don't eat me—"

I stop short. It's not a cat. It's a pigeon. And not just one. There have to be at least ten of them. They waddle in a tight group, their heads bobbing in and out, in and out. "Am I happy to see you guys," I say. I make sure to talk slowly. There's a pigeon named Peggy who hangs around the station sometimes. She's not exactly known for her brains. "I'm looking for 220 Central Park West." No one responds. I make my voice as slow and clear as possible. "Can . . . anyone . . . point . . . me . . . in . . . that . . . direction?"

"I think the rat is slow or somethin'," one of the pigeons snarls.

"He's gotta be to come into pigeon territory," another one snorts.

One pigeon breaks away from the group. He's the largest one, with huge black wings and a proud white chest. "You should know better than to come here." His voice is low and scratchy. He flaps his wings. They beat loudly as he rises into the air. "This dumpster is ours. No food for you here."

He looms above me, more than twice my size. "I just

want to get to 220 Central Park West," I say quickly. "Not to Dumpster Street, wherever that is." The pigeons stare at me. I try talking louder. "220 CENTRAL PARK WEST! MY BROTHER WAS RAT-NAPPED AND I NEED TO FIND—"

"Hey." The large pigeon cuts me off. "We're not *deaf.* And we're not helping any rat. Get outta here."

"But—I—" My mouth hangs open. He must not understand. "I . . . need . . . directions." I say it as slowly as I can.

The pigeon sinks back to the ground, so close that I can smell sour tomato on his beak. He puffs out his snowy white chest. "You really are slow," he jeers.

The other pigeons waddle closer. Their wings brush my back and poke at my tail. "The rat don't wanna leave," one says.

"It's his death wish," says another.

I take a step back. "D-death wish?" I stammer. "No, no death wish here. Only a life wish! Never mind. I'll just, uh, find someone else to ask." I take another step back and bump into more pigeons. They stand wing to wing, glowering down at me.

The large pigeon takes two big waddles, and suddenly he's right in my snout. "I gave you a chance. Now you're not going nowhere." His round, beady eyes meet mine. "Have at 'em, boys," he snarls.

CHAPTER 8

A Deer in Headlights

O w!" I yell. Pigeons peck at my fur and nip at my paws. "Stop that! Let me go!"

The large pigeon laughs. He's standing back, watching. "Who don't love a good rat show?" he snorts.

"Doesn't!" I explode. I gnash my incisors at one pigeon and duck under another's wing. "I think you mean who *doesn't* love a good rat show!" I dart away from the pigeons and scurry into the large green box. It's filled with forages. Familiar smells hit me—crumpled paper and moldy bread and sour tomato. I close my eyes and for a split second I feel like I'm home, foraging in the treasure chest with Oggie.

"Did you not hear me before?"

The scratchy voice makes my eyes pop open.

I'm not home, and I'm not with Oggie. The large

pigeon is perched on the edge of the green box. "I said, this is our dumpster."

Wings flap sharply behind him. I look up. A dozen pigeons circle this thing they call a dumpster. One snaps his beak. Another flashes his talons.

"Please," I gasp. I scramble backward over a bottle and land on a paper plate. "Just let me go."

The large pigeon spreads his wings. He glides silently through the air and lands next to me. "You're not going nowhere," he says. He beats his wings. One hits me in the snout.

I'm thrown backward. I land inside a cracked vat. It's filled with sour tomato sauce. I sink straight to the bottom. Sauce clogs my eyes and goes up my nose. I cough as I paddle my way to the top. I'm coated head to paw in tomato sauce. I smell scrumptious, but I'm too angry to care. "Let me out of here!" I yell. I paw the sauce off my eyes. "I have to get to Central Park West! I have to find my brother!"

The pigeons ignore me. They swarm, flying at me from every side. Talons scratch my snout and wings pound my back. I sink lower into the dumpster, underneath napkins and forks and a whole pile of straws. I swear I catch a whiff of pizza, but then someone shoves me down again. I slip under a can and into some kind of fabric. It smothers my snout and tangles my paws and suddenly I can't move and I can't breathe.

I hear distant laughter. I kick furiously, but it only tangles me up more. I try to breathe, but I just inhale fabric. My chest aches, begging for air. I'm drowning in forages.

"Hey, you hear that?" Another pigeon voice rises above the fray. "Code ER! I hear the garbagemen coming! We gotta go. Now."

"I don't hear—"

"They're coming! Code ER! Code ER!"

There's a flurry of wings. Voices collide above me.

"Outta my way—"

"Move it—"

"I'm not ending up in a trash compactor—"

Their voices fade. Their wings flap into the distance. *Silence.*

They're gone. My paws relax. My head clears. I need to get out of here. I have no idea what garbagemen are, but I'm in no mood to find out.

I bare my incisors and start to gnaw. The fabric tears away in my mouth. I claw my way out and burrow under a stack of cups. I swim through a pool of soda and tunnel through a deliciously moldy vat of mushrooms. Finally I emerge at the top of the dumpster. I climb onto an empty can and suck down big gulps of sweetly rotten air.

If this were one of my stories, I would have beaten the pigeons back single-pawed. But it's not a story. And in real life, I'm not unstoppable at all. I'm completely, utterly *stoppable*.

A sob escapes me as I scramble out of the dumpster. I scurry into a shadow and look around. Darkness is chasing the last bit of light out of the sky. Soon, it will be so dark I'll have to use my whiskers to guide me, and still I'm not any closer to finding Oggie. Another sob racks my body. What was I thinking, going after Oggie all by myself? I have no idea what to do next. I don't even know which direction to turn.

My eyes land on a nearby sewer cover. I choke back another sob as I scurry over to it. There are a few round holes in its cover. I poke my snout through one of them. The stench hits me immediately. Rotten . . . festering . . . rancid . . . Normally, those are some of my favorite smells, but here they're off, all twisted and darkened. They smell of one thing and one thing only. The end.

I stumble backward, coughing. There's only one place that could smell like that. The Roadway. I scurry away as fast as I can and slip back into the shadows. The Roadway is *not* the way to get to my brother. Not if I want to survive the trip.

"Hey, vermin, you dumb enough to still be out here? 'Cause I'm in the mood to kick some rat tail if you are."

I jump at the sound of the voice. I look up and spot a single pigeon in the sky. He has a small black head, a glossy green neck, and white wings striped with black.

There's something strange about the way he's flying. I look more closely. One wing slices cleanly through the air, wide and majestic. The other one wobbles and jerks, short and stumpy. I blink in surprise. He's missing half a wing.

The pigeon flaps his one full wing. He wobbles his one half wing. He soars through the air, lopsided but fast.

I freeze.

He's flying straight toward me.

Chapter 9

Don't Get Your Feathers in a Bunch

I collapse on my side and let my tongue loll out of my snout. It's a trick my dad taught me during sidewalk survival lessons. *If all else fails, play dead.*

The pigeon makes a noisy landing next to me. I keep my eyes squeezed shut. "Hey, you gonna talk to me or what?" the pigeon says. "I can see you breathing. I know you're alive. C'mon, don't get your feathers in a knot."

"The saying is 'don't get your feathers in a *bunch*,'" I grumble.

"I knew you were alive!" says the pigeon.

Oops.

I lift my head reluctantly. I tense, ready to flee. But now that the pigeon is perched right in front of me, I see that he's much smaller than the leader of the flock. I can't help but stare at his jagged half wing. It looks like it was torn right off. "What do you want from me?" I ask.

The pigeon looks around shiftily. "Why're you still here?" he says loudly. "You better get goin' before I . . . uh . . . before I bust you up for real!"

"Fine." I drag myself to my paws. I'm still smudged with tomato sauce, but I can't even muster up the energy to lick myself clean. "I'm going. I don't want to run into any garbagemen anyway." My head droops as I scamper away from the pigeon. I have no idea where to go. Is Central Park West to the right? The left? Straight ahead? How am I supposed to know?

"Hold up," the pigeon whispers.

I look over. The pigeon stretches out his glossy green neck and looks around. "No one else came back, right?"

"Just let me be," I grumble. "I'm leaving, all right?"

"Wait!" the pigeon cries. "Just look behind me," he whispers. "Are there any other pigeons?"

I blow out an angry breath. "No. You're the only one still bothering me."

"Phew." The pigeon shakes out his feathers. His head bobs as he walks toward me. A tremble runs through me, but he doesn't make a move to strike me with his talons. "I'm Kaz," he says. "Well, Kazington, really. But who wants to go by a name that fancy? Nah, I'm just plain ol' Kaz."

I blink at him. His head bobs in a surprisingly friendly way. "You going to tell me your name or what?" he asks.

"I'm Raffie," I say suspiciously. I take a step back. "And I told you, I'm leaving. I know the garbagemen are coming, okay?"

"Nah, we're cool," Kaz says. "I just made that up to save you."

"*Save me?*" I repeat. "But you were the one hurting me!"

"Not me. My flock." A ruffle runs through Kaz's feathers. "They're some nasty birds, am I right? I don't do that violent stuff. But what choice do I have? You got to fly with a flock if you want to survive." Kaz glances around. "They'll be back soon too. We're gonna want to get out of here."

I stare at Kaz. His beady round eyes look nervous. "It's 'going to want to,'" I say with a sniffle.

"What?" Kaz gives me a weird look.

"*Gonna* isn't a word," I explain. "It's '*going to* want to get out of here.'"

Before Kaz can respond, I hear it. Wings. Beating through the air.

"Not good," Kaz says. "Really not good." He waddles in a circle. "We've got to move before they find you."

"Hey, Stumpy!" The voice drifts down from the sky. "Where you at? Get back here or I'm gonna give you another half wing!"

It's the leader of the flock. And he sounds close.

My eyes dart to Kaz's half wing. "Are you . . . ?"

"Yeah," Kaz grumbles. "They call me Stumpy. Because of this." He holds up his half wing and looks around. "Over here." He squeezes under the dumpster, out of sight. I scurry under after him. There's a building next to the dumpster. A human pushes open a door in the back of it, and suddenly amazing smells pour out.

Sweet tomatoes . . .

Doughy crust . . .

Melty cheese . . .

"What's in there?" I breathe.

"That would be a pizza restaurant," Kaz says. "A pretty famous one, if you believe the tourists. Hey, maybe that's where we should go! The flock will never think to look for us in there." He spreads his wings and takes off for the door.

"A restaurant?" I sputter. "You want me to go in a restaurant?" It doesn't matter that it's pizza. It doesn't matter that I'm starving. I heard what my dad said after Grandpa Pax went missing. *He should never have gone in that restaurant. Once he set paw through those doors, he never stood a chance.* "I—I can't," I stammer.

Kaz pauses in the doorway. "I don't like it either, believe me," he says. "But it's this . . . or them."

I look up. The flock of pigeons flies into view. Their wings slice through the air. Their voices melt together: a single, menacing call.

"Don't worry," Kaz says. "I've got a plan." He disappears through the restaurant's door. I swallow hard and scurry after him.

CHAPTER 10

A Little Monkey Business

The smells hit me like a collision. Sauce! Cheese! Crust! They slam into me from every side. The pizza restaurant is the most delicious place I've ever been.

I slip under an empty chair. There are lots of humans here. My heart pounds and my paws shake, but no one is looking at me. They're all looking at Kaz.

He makes a horrible hooting noise as he flies in wild, crooked circles above. The restaurant explodes with voices.

"Look out!"

"Poor guy has a broken wing."

"*¡Cuidado con tu cabeza!*"

"Now thees ees the true New York experience!"

Kaz swoops from table to table, knocking over cups and trampling pizza. I watch enviously as his talons sink into thick, gooey cheese.

"I've got to catch this for my blog." A man jumps up and points his phone at Kaz.

Kaz lands on one of the blades that are spinning on the ceiling, blowing air about. His feathers flap as he spins round and round.

"Is that a *pigeon* on the fan?" A man in a white hat stomps over with a broom. "Uh-uh, not in my restaurant." He grabs the chair I'm hiding beneath and yanks it toward him.

I freeze.

I'm standing in the middle of a restaurant. And I'm completely, totally exposed.

I quiver in place. My dad's voice booms in my head.

Once he set paw through those doors, he never stood a chance.

The man climbs up on the chair. He swings his broom at Kaz. "Go! Get out of here, you filthy bird!" Kaz swoops out of the path of the broom and lands on a woman's head. She leaps up with a shriek.

"Hide, Raffie," Kaz calls over her screams. "I can't keep this distraction up much longer!"

I snap out of my stupor. There's a tall counter in the middle of the restaurant. I race over to it. Behind me, someone shouts, "The bird ees drinking my soda!" I scramble up onto the counter to hide.

My snout drops open. The counter is covered in food. There are huge tubs of sauce and mushrooms and pepperoni. There are thick, fragrant squares of cheese. There's a mound of dough so thick I could tunnel through it. And there's pizza. More pizza than I've ever seen in my life. Full, uneaten pies, all lined up in a row.

Voices swirl around me, but I barely hear them. I only hear the sound of hot, gooey cheese, bubbling on the pizza.

The smell draws me closer. My stomach growls ferociously. I'm so hungry I can't think straight. I need a bite. I creep closer. I open my snout.

"I'm calling the exterminator about that bird," someone says. My head snaps up at the sound of that awful word. A man in a black shirt is moving toward the counter, a phone pressed to his ear. I dive under a pizza pie, out of sight. The crust is warm on top of my back, but I'm shaking too hard to take a nibble. What was Kaz *thinking* bringing us in here? I've got to find a safe way out—before the E word finds me.

I peek out from under the pie. Kaz is flying past the counter. The man in the white hat is running after him. "Get. Out!" the man growls. He slashes his broom at Kaz. Kaz rises out of reach just in time. He circles through the air before landing on the counter. He hops from pie to pie until he's perched next to my hiding spot.

"Great, now all the pies are ruined!" the man with the broom groans. "Is the exterminator coming, Giovanni?"

"He'll be here in five minutes, boss," the man in the black shirt says.

"This bird will be gone by then," the boss growls. "I can promise you that." He stomps toward Kaz, still gripping the broom in his hand.

"Let's get out of here," Kaz says. "My flock should be gone by now."

"Yes, please," I whisper. I peek out farther from under the pizza pie. I'm about to ask how exactly we should do this when my fur starts to prickle. I look up sharply. The boss is staring right at me.

"Is that—Giovanni—holy—*RAT*!" He swings his broom. It comes smashing down, over my head.

"Run, Raffie!" Kaz yells.

I scurry out from under the pizza pie, but cheese drips off it, clinging to my fur. I go skidding along the counter, dragging the pizza with me. "Watch out, Raffie!" Kaz gasps. But it's too late.

The pizza and I both slide off the counter and plummet to the floor.

I land with a thud. My scream is muffled by something soft. I drag myself to my paws. I'm inside a cardboard box, on a bed of napkins. The pizza pie is crumpled next to me. Above me, the broom makes a deafening *crack* as it connects with the counter.

"Don't worry, boss," I hear Giovanni say. "I'll take care of the rat for you." Angry footsteps stomp closer. I dig my claws into the cardboard and climb faster than I ever have in my life. I'm almost out of the box when a huge shadow darkens the air above me. Giovanni.

He's holding something. It looks like a plastic knife I'd find in the treasure chest back home, except it's silver and much, much bigger. He lifts it up. Its long, sharp edge glitters above me. I squeak in terror and lose my grip on the cardboard. I tumble down, back into the box.

"Trapped," I hear Giovanni say gleefully. I right myself just in time to see him throw the knife. Right at me.

I'm walled in by the box. There's nowhere to scurry. Nowhere to escape. The knife whizzes closer.

"Ahhh!" I grab the pizza pie in my paws and hold it in

front of me like a shield. I squeeze my eyes shut. This is it. I'll never get to Oggie. I'll never see my family again. I hear a thunk as the knife pierces the pie and then . . . Nothing.

I open one eye, then the other. The sharp edge of the knife is less than an inch from my snout. The whole thing is stuck, its handle wedged into a slice of pepperoni. My breath comes out in a long, shaky rush.

"Raffie! Are you okay?" Kaz swoops down and perches on the edge of the box. He yanks the knife out of the pizza with his beak.

"Saved by the pizza," I pant.

"Let's go," Kaz says. "Now."

"This pie is coming with us." I sink my teeth into the pizza crust. "In case there are any more knives."

Kaz grabs the other half of the pie in his beak. We move together toward the restaurant's front door, carrying the pizza in our mouths. Battle cries ring through the restaurant.

"Exterminator—"

"—kill—"

"—cool!—"

We move faster. Giovanni shouts something, but I don't look back. Together, we launch ourselves through the restaurant's front door, still carrying the pizza between us.

CHAPTER 11

Not a Clay Pigeon

We stumble down the stairs and across the sidewalk. I duck into a shadow and collapse on my belly, letting the pizza fall to the ground. Kaz stops next to me, panting loudly. The sky stretches above us, black and endless. The last bit of sun is gone, replaced by street lamps. The building next to us winks with lights. A furry figure stands in one of its windows. Two glowing yellow eyes meet mine.

My heart pounds so loudly, I'm sure Kaz can hear it. "Run!" I choke out.

"Again?" Kaz pants. "Is it the exterminator? Where?"

"No, it's . . ." My voice trails off as I watch the cat's sharp claws scratch furiously against the glass. "It's a—a—CAT!"

A laugh mixes in with Kaz's pants. "So what?" he says.

"So *what*?" I sputter. I cower behind Kaz, but I can still see the cat. He's pacing behind the window, drool rolling off his fangs. "To a cat, I'm as delicious as this pizza, Kaz. Maybe even more."

"Then let's get you out of here," Kaz says.

"I couldn't agree more." I grab the pizza in my teeth. Kaz helps me drag it down the block until we find a parked truck to hide under. It's nice and spacious underneath—out of sight of cats and humans and flocks of pigeons.

"What should we do with this?" Kaz nudges the pie with this beak.

My whiskers twitch happily. "What do you think?" I open my snout and dig in. Kaz pecks at the other half. "Scrumptious, right?" I mumble through a mouthful of cheese.

"Well, it's no grass seeds," Kaz says. Crumbs sprinkle out of his beak. "But it's not bad."

When every glob of cheese and speck of crust is gone, I roll onto my back. My belly heaves up and down, stuffed full. "Now I can think," I say.

Kaz stretches out his feathers. "What was all that stuff you said before about your brother?"

I roll back onto my stomach. My paws are still stained with tomato sauce. I busy myself by nibbling it off.

I know what the other rats say about pigeons.

More feathers than brains.

Dumb enough to walk right past a human.

I look up. Kaz is watching me. I nibble at another speck of sauce. Kaz might be a pigeon and he might fly with a nasty flock, but he got me out of that dumpster *and* out of that restaurant. I don't know what he is exactly, but it isn't dumb.

"I'm looking for my little brother," I tell him. And suddenly the words pour out of me. I blurt it all: about my subway station and my parents and Lulu and Oggie, and how I used to tell Oggie these incredible stories, as if I were Raffie the Unstoppable, but they were all made up. "And then Oggie tried to be like me," I say quietly, "and he got stolen away in a cage!"

"Whoa." Kaz shakes his beak. "Those must have been some powerful stories."

I look away, ashamed. "They were just stories," I mutter. I look back at Kaz. "The only good thing is, the boy who took Oggie left a notebook behind. I read the address on it and—"

"You read it?" Kaz cuts in. "Like *read* it? You know how to read?"

I nod. "My parents taught me. It helps us determine the good forages from the bad ones. I'm slow at it, though. You should see my sister, Lulu. She's a reading whiz. But I'm *sure* the notebook said 220 Central Park West." I twitch my tail nervously. "I think that's where Oggie is."

"Central Park," Kaz says dreamily. "That's what first got my attention about you, you know that? You kept talking about Central Park. I always wanted to go there. But I'm not allowed to fly long distances because of my wing." He gives his jagged half wing a flap. "Ziller won't let me."

"Is Ziller your dad?" I ask.

"No." Kaz balks. "He's the leader of my flock. I don't got parents. I mean, I guess I did at one point, but I don't remember them. I've just got Ziller. And he's one nasty bird. You heard him. He calls me Stumpy because of my wing. He'll probably kill me if he finds out I helped you."

"So don't go back to him." I jump to my paws. An idea is pulsing through me. "Come find Central Park with me instead! You said you've always wanted to go there. I can't fly either. We can walk—or, well, waddle— there together."

Kaz cocks his head. For a while, he says nothing. "Wanna know something about pigeons?" he asks finally.

"It's *want to*,'" I correct. "Not *wanna*.'"

Kaz shoots me a look. "I mean yes," I say quickly.

"We pigeons have crazy good senses of direction," Kaz says. "No pigeon will ever get lost, let me tell you that. We've got the sun to guide us. We've got landmarks to lead us. We've got our brain compasses—"

"Your what?" I interrupt.

"Our brain compasses," Kaz repeats. "We can just *feel* in our brains which way to go. It's all to help get us home if we're lost. But . . ." Kaz swishes his wings. "Maybe I can use it to get us to 220 Central Park West instead."

My breath catches in my throat. "What are you saying?" I ask.

"I like you, Raffie. You got good vibes." Kaz snaps his beak thoughtfully. "And there's nothing left for *Stumpy* in this 'hood. I'll come with you. That's what I'm saying."

I'm so excited, I jump up and run a lap around Kaz. "So how do we get there?"

Kaz closes his eyes. He cocks his head. He spreads out his wings and flexes his talons. Finally, he opens his eyes.

"We're not close, I can tell you that," he says. "We'll have to cross a river. Then we'll have to get from the bottom of the city all the way to the top."

My tail droops between my paws. "How do we do that?"

Kaz waddles to the edge of the truck. I scurry over next to him. "There," he says. I look up. Hanging in the dark sky is another floating road. This one has two enormous arches at either end. They glitter with lights as cars zoom beneath them. "Another floating road," I breathe.

"That's called the Brooklyn Bridge," Kaz says. "Humans take it to get over the water, from Brooklyn to Manhattan." Kaz turns to face me. His eyes gleam with excitement. "Maybe we should too."

Brooklyn Arts Photography Contest

Winning Photo!
Title: *The True New Yorkers*
Location: Dumbo, Brooklyn

CHAPTER 12

Don't Chicken Out

I stick close to Kaz as we make our way onto the Brooklyn Bridge. The sky is dark, but lights twinkle above, setting the bridge aglow. My paws tense. I can feel the lights grazing my fur, brightening me up for anyone to see.

I scurry up the railing on the side of the bridge and duck into a shadowy spot. At the other end of the bridge is a long line of buildings. There are so many of them, one after another after another, glittering in a giant constellation of lights. A shiver slides down my back. The city looks so big. A rat could get lost over there.

"I was hoping there wouldn't be lots of people at night, for your sake," Kaz says tightly. "But I guess that's not happening."

I tear my eyes away from the city and look at the long wooden pathway that runs along the center of the bridge.

It's filled with humans. They're walking and running and biking and taking photo after photo. In my shadowy spot on the railing, no one notices me. But the lights only get brighter up ahead. There's no way I'll make it across the whole bridge without being spotted.

Kaz flies in a crooked circle above me. "I think our best bet is to go down there." He points a wing to our right. Below us is another lane, sunken beneath the wooden pathway. It's packed with cars. They creep slowly forward, inching toward the city.

"A traffic jam," Kaz says thoughtfully. He pauses in the air, flapping directly above me. "That gives me an idea." He perches on the railing next to me. "Raffie, I know exactly how we're gonna get into the city."

"Going to," I correct him. "Not *gonna.*"

Kaz snaps his beak impatiently. "Do you want to hear my idea or not?"

I nod.

"We'll hitch a ride!" Kaz announces.

"Itch a ride," I repeat. "Of course. I was thinking the same thing." I scratch at my side with my paw. "Um . . . exactly how itchy do we need to be?"

"Nah, not itch. *Hitch.* It means we're gonna borrow a ride," Kaz explains.

"Going to," I say again.

The feathers on Kaz's neck ruffle. "What does it matter?"

"I . . . well . . ." I curl my tail in my front paws. "It just *does*," I sputter. "I tell stories, Kaz. And in a story, every word is important."

I look down, thinking of the last time I told Oggie exactly that. It was just the other night. We were curled up in my shoe box together, and I was telling him a Raffie the Unstoppable story. It was my most exciting one yet: Raffie the Unstoppable had just escaped the E word—only to end up stuck in the Roadway. "There were rattraps and poison at every turn," I told Oggie in a hushed voice. "Raffie the Unstoppable was worried he'd finally met his demise."

"Don't chicken up, Raffie the Unstoppable!" Oggie gasped.

I stopped the story to correct him. "The saying is 'don't chicken *out*,'" I informed him.

"So?" Oggie said. "I was close enough, right?"

I shook my snout. "It's like I'm always telling you, Oggie. Every word is important."

Oggie nodded and snuggled closer. I could feel his little heart beating against my fur. "Okay, don't chicken out, Raffie the Unstoppable!" he cheered.

My throat closes up tight at the memory. I take a deep breath and turn my focus back to Kaz.

"Fine," he says, with a shrug of his wings. "We're *going to* hitch a ride. Better?"

"Much." I pause. "But, um . . . what exactly does that involve?"

"All we've got to do is sneak inside a car," Kaz explains. "It can't be that hard. I've heard chipmunks talking about doing it and we all know how lazy chipmunks are—"

"Wait," I interrupt. "Did you just say 'inside'? Actually *inside* a car? With a human?"

Kaz nods. "That's how you do it."

My stomach turns. I can think of about a hundred things that can go wrong in that scenario. But I hear Oggie's voice in my head. *Don't chicken out, Raffie the Unstoppable!* I take a deep breath. Oggie is somewhere over that bridge. I have to get to him. "Okay," I say. "How do we do this?"

"We need to look for two things," Kaz instructs. "An open window and a backseat with no heads bobbing in it."

We're both quiet as we scan the cars crawling past. A silver van has all its windows shut. A bright yellow car has an open window, but three heads bob in the back. A rusty, white car wobbles past. Smoke curls up behind it. Its windows are open, and the backseat is empty. "How about that one?" I suggest.

"Nah." Kaz shakes his beak. "That's one old nasty car."

"It's called vintage," I say knowingly. My gaze lands

on a long black car. Its back windows are open, and I don't see a single head bobbing behind the driver. "There's one," I exclaim.

Kaz flies into the air to get a better look. "That's good," he says. "Real good. It's a limousine, which means it's got a window separating the front seat from the back seat. The driver won't suspect a thing."

Kaz flies down to the car lane. He twists his head back to look at me. "Come on," he yells.

I start down the railing. It's so bright up here, I feel like I'm on display. Down below, the line of cars inches forward. A driver looks out his window. His eyes land on me. His eyebrows shoot up, and I swear I can hear his battle cry, even from all the way up here. I try to move, but it's like my run-in with the thief all over again. I can't move my legs. I can't move my tail. I can't even breathe.

"What's taking so long, Raffie?" Kaz flies over. His wings flap in front of me, blocking me from the man's view. "Hurry or we'll miss the limo!"

I draw in a shaky breath as I look up at Kaz. It's not the same as with the thief. This time, I'm not alone. "Fly in front of me," I instruct. I scurry down the rest of the way with Kaz protecting me from sight. I blow out a sigh of relief when my paws hit asphalt. But the instant I see the cars, I freeze up all over again.

I've seen cars back home, of course, but I've never

been this close to them. I'm so close I can smell the humans inside. The cars are monstrous. One run-in with a tire and I'd be flatter than a juice box on the subway tracks. "I'm not sure this is such a good idea," I say.

"Nah, it's a great idea." Kaz nudges me forward with his beak. "We both want to get to Central Park, right? Well, this will make it easier." Next to us, the cars screech to a standstill.

"Now's our chance to get close to the limo." Kaz pushes me forward again. Suddenly I'm snout to metal with the limo door. "We just need to get through the window," he says.

I look up. Between the open window and me is a long stretch of shiny, smooth metal. I paw nervously at it, testing it out. Metal is the hardest material to get a grip on—especially when it's this smooth.

The car moves forward. The tire just barely misses my tail. I leap backward. My heart is thudding so wildly I can feel it all the way down in my paws. "I—I can't do this," I call up to Kaz. My voice sounds strange, all high-pitched and strangled. "I don't have wings to fly me up to that window, and if I try to climb the door, I'm going to slip and fall and get crushed under a tire. I can't get to Oggie if I'm nothing more than a splatter on the Brooklyn Bridge!" The last part comes out a little more like a scream than a sentence.

Kaz cocks his head thoughtfully. "I got this." He

swoops downward and stretches out his talons. "Grab on," he says.

"Grab on?" I repeat. The limo moves forward with a lurch. I back even farther away.

"Hurry!" Kaz says. His talons dangle above me.

I'm shaking all over as I lift onto my hind legs and latch on to Kaz's talons. He rises slowly into the air, taking me with him. We wobble to the left. We wobble to the right. I look down. The ground is suddenly far beneath us.

Kaz grunts as he flies toward the limo's open window. "Hold on tight," he says. He dives in beak first. I tumble in after him. His talons slip from my grip. I go plummeting down for the second time that night.

I crash into a seat. My snout is smushed against leather. My tail is jammed under a belt. Slowly, I pull myself up. I spit out a mouthful of seat lint. "You okay?" I mumble. I turn around to find Kaz.

Instead, I find myself looking at the tiniest, prissiest dog I've ever seen. She has fluffy white fur, a sparkly pink collar, and nails painted pink to match. Her tiny snout is perfectly trimmed and her long, pouffy ears stink like roses. Slowly, she lifts her head off her silky, pink pillow. "Did you *really* just interrupt my beauty sleep?" she sniffs.

CHAPTER 13

Let Sleeping Dogs Lie

A re you *seriously* in my limo right now?" The dog skitters backward in her silk bed. Her sparkly collar glitters. "No way." She waves a paw at me. "Just, go. Be gone!"

"But we need a ride," I say. I give her my best wide-eyed, whisker-quivering pout, the one that gets me out of slop cleanup at home. "My name is Raffie and my friend Kaz and I are trying to get to Central Park West to save—"

"Um, did you not hear me?" the dog interrupts. "I se-riously cannot have you two in my limo. Do you know who I am? I'm Marigold Rose Valencia the Third, blue-ribbon winning show dog and star of the reality TV show *Trust Fund Dog*. Mouse stench does *not* belong in my limo."

"Mouse?" I exclaim. "Did you just call me a—" I stop short. My fur is bristling all over from her insult, but I need this dog's help. I clear my throat. "Excuse me," I say. I use my sweetest voice. "It's just that I'm actually a rat."

"Mouse, rat, *whatever*," Marigold snaps. "Just leave the way you came in, or I'll call my chauffeur to save me. 'Kay?"

"The only thing you need saving from is that hairstyle," Kaz says. He climbs up from where he landed on the floor of the car. His beak is smudged with dirt, and his feathers are rumpled.

"My fur is perfection, thank you very much." Marigold tosses her fluffy ears. "It better be. I just spent eight hours at Brooklyn's Prestigious Pampered Poodle Spa. I was bathed in a rose-scented bubble bath. I was fluff-dried by a state-of-the-art blow-dryer. I was massaged and combed, pouffed and coiffed, manicured and perfumed." She looks appraisingly from me to Kaz. "Which is why I look like this and you both look like . . . that." She sniffs at the air. "Hashtag *pee-yew*."

"Hash browns?" I ask eagerly. "Where?" I sniff at the air. "Are they all squishy and spoiled?"

Marigold scrunches up her snout. "The only thing that smells spoiled here is you. Please tell me you know what a bath is."

"Of course I do," I scoff. "I just took one two weeks ago. The rainwater that drips onto the subway tracks is the perfect temperature for a nice, relaxing bath."

Marigold makes a strange gagging noise. She probably ate a button by mistake. That's happened to me before. They look a lot like olives, but they do not taste the same.

"Listen," Kaz says. "We need a ride. Can we just hitch for a few minutes?" He shakes out his rumpled feathers. One floats across the car and lands on Marigold's bed.

"Pigeon cooties!" Marigold gasps. "I've got the pigeon cooties! Do you know what you've just done? Now that I've lost Rex, my beauty is all I have left!" She paws frantically at her fur and shakes out her ears at the same time. She looks just like Lulu did that time she accidentally stuck her paw in an electric socket.

I try not to laugh. I really do. But a tiny giggle slips out.

Marigold's head snaps up. "Don't you dare LOL at me," she growls.

I quickly squeeze my eyes shut and cover my ears with my paws. Good thing Lulu taught me what LOL stands for. "I'm not looking or listening!" I say. "Can we have a ride now?"

But with my ears covered, I can't hear her answer. I open one eye a tiny bit. Marigold is lifting her lips to show me her teeth. They're straight and tiny and shiny white. She must want to see my teeth in return. I've never understood dog behavior. They *choose* to lick humans. But I need this dog to like me, so I flash my incisors at her. Those are my very best teeth. I can gnaw through almost anything with them.

Kaz knocks me with his wing. "Shut your snout," he whispers. "Do you wanna get a ride or not?"

"There is no ride to get," Marigold huffs. "Leave right

now, or I'll alert my chauffeur, Thomas. I've spent the last five years training him. All I have to do is give a single howl of fear, and he will pull over the car. 'Kay?"

Kaz and I both look at the window that separates the front of the car from the back. It's shut tight, and the human in the front is nodding his head to music. "You mean that guy behind the window?" Kaz snorts. "You've been making noise this whole time, and he hasn't seemed to notice."

"That's because I haven't been loud enough," Marigold insists. "He's very well trained. Humans are totally intelligent animals, you know. They can be taught to do over one hundred tricks." Marigold tosses her fluffy white ears. "Watch. I can prove it to you. Do you want some food?"

At the sound of my favorite word, my stomach grumbles. The pizza already feels like a long time ago. "I could eat," I say.

"'Kay, ready?" Marigold stands up tall and throws back her head. "Food now!" she yaps loudly.

In the front seat, the driver reaches for something. Without looking back, he opens the window, tosses it into the backseat, and shuts the window.

"Hashtag I told you so," Marigold says. She kicks the food over to me. I was hoping for a nice, spoiled hash brown, but this is shaped like a chicken bone. It smells weird, all dry and chalky. But my stomach is grumbling, so I gobble it up. It's not very good, but at least it's stale.

"Do you know what happens if two lowlifes like you are found bothering a high-class animal like *me*?" Marigold asks. She lowers her voice to a whisper. I have to lean in to hear her. "Animal Control, that's what."

I shiver. I've heard stories about Animal Control. Animals go in and they never come out.

"You've got three seconds," Marigold warns. "Then I'll get Thomas. And he'll get Animal Control."

Not Just Puppy Love

"O ne," Marigold counts.

Kaz nudges me with his stubby wing. "Let's go," he grumbles. "This dog is crazier than humans in rush hour. We'll find another way into Manhattan."

I glance out the window. We're already near the end of the bridge. If I can just keep Marigold talking, we might stand a chance at making it into the city.

"Two," Marigold continues.

"Who's Rex?" I blurt out.

"None of your business," Marigold snaps. "Three—"

"Wait!" I think of Oggie somewhere in that big, bright city, trapped in his cage. What if he's hungry? What if the humans are hurting him? What if—I swallow hard— what if they've already called in the E word? Or Animal Control? My fur bristles all over. "I really want to know who Rex is," I say desperately. On the other side of the window, the buildings of Manhattan creep closer. I have to keep her talking.

"Is he your brother?" I ask. "I have a brother. That's who we're trying to save. His name is Oggie, and he's the sweetest, cutest rat anyone's ever known." Thinking about Oggie makes me feel all choked up, like I accidentally ate a whole shoelace. A sob rises inside me, but I take a deep breath and shove it back down. "He loves when I tell him stories," I continue, "and he always wants to do everything I do, and—"

"Rex is not my brother," Marigold says impatiently. "If you really have to know, he's the love of my life!" She collapses in a fluffy heap and buries her head in her paws.

"And that's a bad thing?" Kaz asks.

Marigold looks up with a sigh. "My human-mom doesn't approve of Rex. It's because . . . well . . ." She lowers her voice to a whisper. "He's a *mutt*." She moans softly. "I know what you're thinking. What is a beautiful specimen like Marigold Rose Valencia the Third doing with a . . . a . . . *you know*?"

"Not even close to what I was thinking," Kaz mutters. I kick him in the talon. My plan is working! The longer we can keep Marigold talking, the better.

"You read my mind, Marigold," I jump in. "Tell us how that happened. I want to hear every detail."

"Are you *trying* to die of boredom?" Kaz whispers in my ear. I nudge him in the side and point my snout toward the city. The towering buildings are closer than ever. "Oh." Kaz turns to Marigold. "Raffie's right. We need to hear every detail."

Marigold slowly sits up. "Well . . ." She sniffles. "I guess it all started when our housekeeper began taking me to the basement with her when she did our laundry. I used to seriously hate it—I mean, she'd make me ride on top of the hamper! Who wants to smell like dirty laundry? But then one day, I met Rex."

"His human-father is our building's super. Which means he fixes stuff around the building. Hashtag super handy. They live in an apartment in the basement. At first I was like, *ew*, mutt! But Rex is so big and strong. He scared off that awful old Mrs. Pilly-Wink with a single growl, and she'd been mussing up my fur for years! Always petting my head like I'm some common lapdog. Plus, he could push the laundry room door open with just his nose. He just made me *feel* things, you know? I don't care what anyone says. It wasn't just puppy love."

"Puppy love?" I repeat.

"Like some silly young crush," Marigold huffs.

"Puppy love," I murmur. I mentally store the phrase away to tell Oggie later.

"Then one day," Marigold continues, "our housekeeper

caught Rex and I canoodling behind the boiler. She told my human-mom, and I've been banned from the laundry room ever since. I didn't even get a chance to tell Rex." She shakes her head, making her fluffy ears swing from side to side. "He probably thinks I forgot about him. Or found someone else. But there's no one else for me," she whimpers. "If only my human-mom knew Rex like I do. He's such a gentleman. Every Saturday when he goes to Central Park, he carries a flower back for me in his teeth. He has good taste in flowers, too, none of those ugly dandelions, which are really just weeds—"

"Wait." My breath catches in my throat. "Did you say Central Park? Do you live near there?"

"Of course not." Marigold sniffs. "Uptown is totally overrated. I live in Gramercy."

"But Rex goes to Central Park?" I press.

"Every Saturday, with his human-dad." Marigold looks out the window. "I miss those flowers—"

"I need to talk to Rex!" I cut in. I'm so excited that my whiskers stick straight out. "I need to ask him the best way for an animal to get to Central Park."

The car bumps as it rumbles off the bridge. I look out the window. Huge green signs dangle from poles. Buildings clog up the sky. We're officially in Manhattan. "You have to help us get to Rex," I beg Marigold.

"Um, no, I don't," Marigold sniffs. "He's the love of *my* life. Why should you get to see him when I can't?"

I think quick. "That's exactly why. If we can reach Rex, we can talk to him for you."

Marigold's tail lifts. She cocks her head. "You could give him a message?" she asks slowly.

I nod. "Whatever you want."

Marigold looks out the window. The streets are so bright with lights here, you can barely tell it's night-time. "'Kay, fine," she says. "I'll help. But I'm warning you. Rex's human-dad could be down there with him. And he's totally declared war on rats."

I fidget on my paws. The city zips past outside, packed with humans and cars and buildings that are taller than any I've ever seen. This is only a tiny section of the city, and already it feels like it never ends. Fear gnaws at my stomach, sharp as incisors. I look at Kaz. "Can your brain compass get us to Central Park?"

"It will help me sense the right direction," Kaz says. "But it's not a guidebook or anything. We have to figure out the route."

I take a deep breath and sit up tall. "I don't care about Rex's human-dad," I declare. "Oggie's lost, and I have to find him. We'll do whatever it takes to get to Central Park."

"Whatever it takes," Kaz agrees. He gives his wings an excited flap. "I've been dreaming of this my whole life."

I try to ignore the fear gnashing at my insides as we wind through the city streets. We're moving fast now. The city spins past outside, one building blending into the next. Still, even blurred together like that, things look different here: bigger, taller, shinier. I know Brooklyn can't be that far away, but it feels like it's on the other side of the world. I lose track of time as one street turns into another and then another until I'm so dizzy I have to close my eyes.

Finally, the car glides to a stop. I scurry over to look out the window. We're next to the tallest, shiniest building I've ever seen. It goes up and up and up. Trees grow out of the very top of it.

"What is this place?" I whisper.

"This," Marigold says smugly, "is home sweet home."

I glance at Kaz. His beak is chattering nervously. I ignore the trembling in my paws as I turn back to Marigold. "Tell us how to get to Rex."

CHAPTER 15

In the Doghouse

The front door of the car swings open. "Ooh, I have an idea!" Marigold squeals. "Get in my bag, 'kay?" She nods at a pink sparkly bag in the corner of the seat.

Kaz immediately backs away. "Uh-uh. No way. I don't do small spaces."

Footsteps make their way around the side of the car. "Thomas is coming," Marigold says. "Hurry!"

"Please, Kaz," I beg. "I'll be right there with you."

Kaz backs farther away. His wings flatten against his sides. "I—I can't."

The footsteps draw closer. "Now!" Marigold hisses.

I look from the bag to Kaz. I don't have a choice. "Sorry, Kaz." I rush toward him and sink my teeth into his tail.

He flaps forward with a yelp of pain—straight toward the bag. "Ow! What did you do that for?"

I don't answer. I just ram my whole body into his. With another flap, Kaz goes stumbling into Marigold's bag. I scurry in after him just as the door to the backseat flings open. "Time to get in your bag, Marigold," I hear a deep voice say.

Marigold squeezes in behind us. She pulls the bag's door shut with her teeth. "Stay behind me," she whispers. "And get under the blanket."

I grab Marigold's silky pink blanket and throw it over Kaz. I squeeze under next to him. "I'm sorry—" I begin, but I stop when I see the look on his face. He doesn't look mad. He looks terrified.

"Is it me or are the walls closing in on us?" he asks shakily.

Before I can answer, the bag is jerked into the air. I'm flung backward against the pink, sparkly wall. Jewels stab at my snout. Sequins scrape my fur.

Distantly, I hear the chauffeur let out a grunt. "What did they feed you at the groomer, Marigold? *Bricks?*"

I scramble to my paws and spit out a mouthful of pink glitter. "You okay, Kaz?" I whisper.

Kaz is lying on his side. He flaps his wings to right himself. Sequins and feathers rain down around him. "I am not in this bag," he murmurs, squeezing his eyes shut. "I'm in the wide, open sky, stretching out my wings . . ."

"Just don't stretch them too far, 'kay?" Marigold says over her shoulder. "I do *not* need more pigeon feathers on me." She curls up in a tiny ball at the front of the bag. "Or rat fur," she adds pointedly.

"You're the one who made us get into this death trap," Kaz says without opening his eyes. He's breathing hard, his wings heaving up and down.

"Tell me about it." Marigold sighs. "The things you do in the name of love."

I peek out through the bag's small mesh window. We're

outside now. Everything moves so fast here. Cars and bikes and humans whiz past. They must all be really hungry to be in such a hurry, I decide. I look away, feeling dizzy. Kaz's eyes are still closed, and he's murmuring to himself about open skies.

"What's the plan?" I ask Marigold.

Marigold sits up. "When we get inside the lobby, Sal the doorman will want to say hello to me." She lifts her nose in the air. "He doesn't get to meet a lot of celebrities, you know. So Thomas will put down the bag and take me out to say hi. That's your cue. Sal and Thomas will be distracted by my beauty. So you'll have a chance to escape. Go straight to the back of the lobby. Behind the row of plants. I'll keep the humans distracted long enough for you to get there. There's a stairwell to the basement back there. The door's broken and doesn't totally close. There should be enough space for you two to squeeze through."

I look over at Kaz, hoping he's listening. He's the one with the supernatural direction skills. But his eyes are still shut tight. "Clouds brush against my wings . . ." he murmurs.

I turn back to Marigold. "Tell me one more time," I say.

Thomas stops short in front of a tall glass door. The bag bounces against his side. This time, I dig my claws into the bottom to keep from being tossed around.

Marigold repeats the plan as the door glides open. A blast of cool air rushes into the bag. It smells disgustingly sweet, like the liquid the thief scrubs around our station after he robs us.

"Whatever you do, don't forget my message," Marigold finishes. "Tell Rex I love him and to find a way to get to me. And tell him . . ." She drops her head. Her voice comes out in a shy whisper. "Tell him I miss his pawsy wawsies."

"His pawsy *what*?" I say.

Marigold's fur bristles. "Pawsie wawsies," she snaps.

"Got it," I reply with a giggle.

I press my snout to the mesh window again. I can see the lobby on the other side. My eyes go wide. Everything gleams. The walls, the doors, even the floor. It's shinier than the subway tracks after a storm. It's enough to make me lose my appetite. "Why is it so *clean* in here?" I whisper.

"It's a luxury building, of course," Marigold huffs. "But watch out when you get to the basement. The Seven Deadly Scums are down there." Marigold shudders. "I've spotted all of them: dust, dirt, mud, mold, rot, dung, and grime."

My stomach yawns hungrily. I've never heard of scum, but it sounds delicious.

"Welcome back," a deep voice booms outside the bag. "Let me see our pretty little Marigold."

"That's Sal the doorman," Marigold whispers. "Hurry. Get back under the blanket."

I yank the blanket over us. Then I pop back out. "Marigold, wait," I whisper.

"What's your problem?" Marigold snaps. "Thomas is coming!"

"It's just . . . well . . . thank you," I say quickly. "For helping us."

"Oh." Marigold's eyes meet mine. "Well, you're not that bad. For a rat. Just remember to give my message to Rex!"

I slip back under the blanket. "Keep quiet," I whisper to Kaz. His eyes dart frantically back and forth, but he keeps his beak shut.

"Come out and say hi, Marigold," Thomas says cheerfully.

The bag drops onto the ground, knocking me into Kaz. I pull the blanket more tightly around us. There's a tiny hole where the threads in the blanket have worn thin. Through it, I watch the bag's door drop open. I hold my breath. Next to me, Kaz tenses.

A large human hand reaches into the bag.

CHAPTER 16

A Dog and Pony Show

The hand reaches farther into the bag. An eye peers in next to it. "Come on out, Marigold," Thomas says. "Sal wants to see you."

His hand freezes. His voice falls silent. "What's with the mess, Marigold? How did you manage to knock all those sequins off? And is that a *feather*?"

His hand reaches past Marigold . . .

. . . straight toward us.

My heart beats wildly.

The hand comes closer.

Closer.

I tremble against Kaz. Thomas's hand is going to find us and then it will be all battle cries and Animal Control and—

Marigold leaps on top of Thomas's hand. "Take me out!" she howls. "Right now!"

"One second, Marigold." Thomas tries to shake her off, but she digs her claws in, holding on tight.

"Ow, stop it, Marigold," Thomas says impatiently. "I want to clean this out . . ."

Marigold begins furiously licking Thomas's fingers. I try not to gag. I will never understand dogs.

"That tickles." Thomas giggles. Marigold licks him faster. "All right, all right, I'll clean the bag later. Come say hi to Sal." Thomas's fingers wrap around Marigold's back. His hand pulls out of the bag.

Marigold twists around. "Don't forget my message!" she calls out. Then Thomas carries her out of sight.

I push the blanket off. We don't have a lot of time.

Kaz is huddled in a ball, his beak chattering loudly. Outside the bag, I hear Sal's booming voice. "Look how spiffy you are, Marigold, all nice and groomed!"

They're distracted by her beauty. This is our chance.

"Run!" I exclaim.

Kaz leaps to his talons. "Don't have to tell me twice," he wheezes. His wings knock into me as he barrels out of the bag. I scurry after him.

"Marigold is doing tricks!" I hear Sal say behind us. We hurry away from the humans while they're distracted.

"Marigold said we have to get behind the row of plants," I whisper.

"Those plants?" Kaz asks.

I follow his gaze to a long line of plants. All the way on the other side of the room. I swallow hard. "Those plants," I confirm.

Kaz lifts his wings, but I shake my head.

"Too loud," I say. "You're going to have to run with me."

We race across the lobby's shiny tile floor. Kaz pants as he waddles beside me. Behind us, I hear Marigold putting on a show to distract the humans. "Look how high I can leap!" she yaps.

Kaz and I duck behind a large white bath as we hurry on. The water spouting out of it is so clear it doesn't have even a tinge of rust. "Who would want to bathe in *that*?" I whisper.

"Are you kidding?" Kaz pants. "Nothing's better than a fountain for a good birdbath." We round a bend. We're out of sight of Thomas and Sal. I sigh in relief. "Almost there." Kaz pants.

Ding!

I jump at the sound of the high-pitched noise. "What was that?" I whisper.

"Elevator," Kaz gasps. A silver door in the wall slides open. An old woman limps out on a cane.

"Hide!" I squeak. We dive side by side toward the plants.

A shriek rings out behind us. "Holy kitten caboodles! It's a—a—AHHHHH!"

My stomach drops all the way to my paws. We've been seen.

CHAPTER 17

Not a Spring Chicken Anymore

Ahh!" the old lady rasps. "A—a—a MOUSE!"

I skid to a stop. "What did you call me?" I spin around. Blood pounds in my ears. I see Kaz out of the corner of my eyes, but I can't hear what he's saying. All I hear is that awful word.

Mouse.

I lash my tail. "Would a mouse have a tail this strong? Or teeth this sharp? Or—ow!" Something stabs at my tail.

"Payback," Kaz says. He clamps his beak around my tail and flaps his wings. He rises into the air, bringing me with him. My stomach seizes. I'm dangling upside down, hanging by my tail.

Kaz flies crookedly over the line of plants. I swing through the air. Leaves and flowers spin beneath me.

Behind us the woman shrieks again. "There's also a—a—PIGEON! GET OUT!"

The woman swings her cane. It smashes into Kaz from behind. "My wing!" he moans. He tilts to the side. I jerk wildly beneath him.

"Hurt . . ." Kaz pants. "Can't . . . stay . . . up . . ."

We lurch to the left. We lurch to the right. We go spiraling down. The floor rushes up to meet us. "Oh no," I gasp. "We're going to—"

We crash down hard. I'm flattened against the floor. Pain shoots from my head to my paws. On the other side of the plants, the woman's shrieks grow louder. I hear pounding footsteps, and then Sal the doorman's booming voice. "What's wrong, Mrs. Pilly-Wink?"

"Hide," Kaz rasps. I peel myself off the ground. Every inch of my body aches, but I drag myself into the largest plant I can find. Kaz limps in behind me. Big yellow flowers bloom on its branches. We duck underneath them. Their sweet stench is so awful I have to cover my snout with my paws.

"What took you so long, young man?" Mrs. Pilly-Wink scolds. "I could be dying over here!"

"Are you?" Sal gasps.

"Well, of course not, but something nearly as bad happened. I saw a mouse! And a pigeon! *Inside* the building."

"Did you now?" Sal asks kindly.

"I did! They were right here. The mouse was squeaking and the pigeon was hooting and then the pigeon picked the mouse up by his tail and flew him over there!"

"Behind the plants?" Sal asks. A shadow looms over us. I burrow deeper under the flowers and try not to gag. "I don't see anything," Sal says.

"They were right there!" Mrs. Pilly-Wink insists. "I got them with my cane!"

"Okay, I'll look for them," Sal says gently. "You go on your way, and I'll be sure to take care of it."

"Don't leave this area," Mrs. Pilly-Wink commands. "They have to be here somewhere."

"Of course," Sal says. "Now you have a good night, you hear?"

Mrs. Pilly-Wink grumbles something in return. Then her uneven footsteps move away, punctuated by the clunk of a cane. "Bye, Mrs. Pilly-Wink!" Sal calls after her.

A new, heavier set of footsteps makes its way over. "Everything okay?" I recognize the voice. It's Thomas, Marigold's chauffeur. "Sorry it took me so long. I couldn't get Marigold back in her bag. I don't know what's gotten into her tonight."

"Everything's fine." Sal sighs. "Just Mrs. Pilly-Wink. She's not a spring chicken anymore. Poor gal must have forgotten to take her medicine again. Says she saw a pigeon flying back here, carrying a mouse in its beak. Can you imagine?"

Sal chuckles, and Thomas joins in. "Well, I better get Marigold home," Thomas says. "See you later, Sal."

As he walks away, I hear the muffled sound of Marigold yapping in her bag. "It was a pigeon and a *rat*, 'kay? And while we're at it . . ."

There's a sharp *ding*, and Marigold's voice fades to nothing.

"A pigeon and a mouse," Sal murmurs. He chuckles again. "Poor old Mrs. Pilly-Wink."

CHAPTER 18

A Dog-Eat-Dog World

I wait for Sal's footsteps to retreat before I stand up. I shake out my paws one by one. I'm sore, but my paws are still working. I turn to Kaz. He's leaning on his side. The green feathers on his neck are flared, and his full wing looks funny. "Are you okay?" I whisper.

Slowly, Kaz lifts his full wing. He makes it halfway up before he gasps out in pain and lets it flop back against his side.

"Is it . . . ?" I can't even finish the sentence. We'll never make it to Central Park West if Kaz has a broken wing.

Kaz tries again. His feathers ruffle with pain, but this time he lifts his wing all the way. He blows out a breath as he lowers it back down. "It's just bruised," he says. "I'm not gonna be able to fly for a bit, but it will get better."

I collapse on a yellow flower. I'm so relieved I barely even notice its awful stench. Kaz peeks out through a gap in the leaves. "Elevator's opening again," he whispers. "We'll just have to wait for the coast to clear." He shifts, and a moan of pain escapes him.

"I'm so sorry, Kaz," I whisper. "This is all my fault. The woman called me a mouse and I just . . . I got so mad that I forgot everything else."

Kaz focuses his round, beady eyes on me. "What's so bad about mice, anyway?"

"Have you ever seen a mouse?" I blurt out. "They're weak! And they can barely gnaw through anything! And they're just . . . so *tiny*!"

"Dude, you're tiny," Kaz says.

"And I hate it!" I explode. I lower my voice. "I'm smaller than all the girl rats! And big rats like Ace are always beating me to the good forages. I just . . ." My whiskers quiver angrily. "I want to be a normal rat."

Slowly, Kaz sits up. He grunts with pain as he waddles closer. "Do you think I asked for this wing?" He lifts his stubby wing. It's half the size of his full wing, with a jagged edge. I shake my snout. "Of course I didn't," Kaz says. "But you don't get to pick who you are. You only get one choice in the matter, and that's how you feel about it. Are you gonna like you? Or are you gonna hate you? That's it. Your only choice." Kaz gives his stumpy wing a flap. "I'll tell you," he continues. "Liking is a whole lot easier than hating. Besides, half a wing is better than no wing, right?"

"I guess." I lick at my sore paws. "How did that happen to your wing, anyway?"

"Ziller found me like this when I was a baby." Kaz leans against a branch with a groan. "He said a falcon must have attacked me."

I flinch as my tongue hits a sore spot on my paw. "Does it hurt?"

"Nah. It just makes me fly funky." Kaz cocks his head. "Does being small hurt?"

"Of course not," I say.

"There you go," Kaz says. "You can't hate something that doesn't hurt, am I right?"

I keep my eyes on my paws. I don't know how to explain it to Kaz. If I'd been large enough to save that pizza from Ace, Oggie would have never left home. He would have never been rat-napped. I would have never had to run away. We'd be on the subway platform right now, foraging for food together. I lick harder at my paws. Being small doesn't make me hurt on the outside. It makes me hurt on the inside. And it hurts the people I love, too.

I clear my throat. "Do you remember your home before Ziller found you?" I ask, changing the subject.

"Not really." Kaz stretches out his talons. "Just this one thing. I remember a branch. It was real nice and thick. It forked into two, and it had a nest tucked into the crook of it." He shrugs his wings, then flinches in pain. "But maybe I just made that up in my head. Ziller says he's got no clue what I'm talking about."

"It sounds like a memory to me," I say. I peek through a gap in the flowers. The elevator doors are closed. There are no humans in sight. "Coast is clear."

"We better hurry," Kaz says.

I scurry out of the plant. Kaz limps out after me. There's a large wooden door nearby. The wood is warped, so it doesn't close all the way. "That's it," I whisper.

We squeeze through the opening. The stairwell is dark and narrow. I scurry down. Kaz moans a little as

he follows. The stairwell leads to a dingy room with low ceilings. I take a deep breath. The aroma of dirt and rust fills my nostrils. "Now that's more like it," I say.

"Well, well, well," someone growls. "Look what we have here."

I spin around. A dog is standing across the room. But this is no tiny, pampered Marigold dog. This dog is massive. He's nearly as wide as a door, with paws so large they could squash me in a single step. His tail is short and thick, his fur is coarse and dark, and he's wearing a sharp, spiked collar around his neck. This must be Rex.

Rex snarls, baring his large, gleaming teeth. Drool runs down the side of his snout. "Perfect timing," he growls. "I was hoping for an evening snack." He unhinges his jaw and lunges right at us.

CHAPTER 19

Every Dog Has Its Day

Wait!" I squeak. "We're friends of Marigold's!"

The dog skids to a stop in front of us. He's so close I can feel his hot, chalky breath. A line of drool swings from his mouth. He shakes his head, and the drool sprays everywhere. Droplets rain down, soaking into my fur.

"Marigold?" he snarls. "I haven't heard from her in weeks. And back when I knew her, she wouldn't be caught dead with a rat or a pigeon."

"Are you Rex?" I ask.

"That's Mr. Rex to you." Rex snaps his jaw. His teeth flash, huge and sharp. "I like a little respect from my meals."

"Marigold wants you to know she still loves you!" My heart's rattling so loudly, I'm sure he can hear it. "She asked us to tell you."

"She wants you to find a way to get to her," Kaz adds. His voice is tense with pain. His wing hangs limply at his side. I scoot in front of him. If Rex wants to eat Kaz, he'll have to get through me first.

"It's true," I plead. "Marigold misses you. Heart emoji!" I add. I picked that up on the subway platform recently. It's fancy human talk for love.

Rex cocks his head. "I don't buy it," he growls. "And I'm really hungry, so . . ." He gnashes his teeth.

"There was another message," Kaz says. "What was it, Raffie?"

I try to dredge it up, but my brain goes blank. Everything darkens around me. All I see are Rex's huge, white fangs.

"I do love a warm snack," Rex growls.

Kaz is talking, but his voice sounds distant. "She misses your tail . . . No, it was your fur . . ."

Rex lunges.

His mouth opens around me. Razor-sharp teeth graze my fur. Huge paws knock into me. "Pawsy wawsies!" I gasp. Adrenaline pumps though me, bringing the world back into focus. "That's it! That's what Marigold misses!"

Rex freezes. His mouth is locked around my back. Pinpricks of pain shoot through me.

"He's right," Kaz jumps in. "Marigold said she misses your pawsy wawsies, Mr., um, Rex, sir . . ."

Slowly, Rex lifts his head. His teeth slide off me. "You really do know my Maripoo," he breathes.

"That's what we've been telling you," Kaz says.

Rex's tail wags. "My Maripoo," he blubbers. "She still loves me!" He opens his mouth and pounces at me.

I cry out in surprise. He's still going to eat me.

"Please," I beg. I squeeze my eyes shut, unable to look. "I'm not very tasty! Eat some pizza instead!"

Something soft and wet strokes my back. I open my eyes. A huge, pink tongue lolls over me. Rex is licking me. "My Maripoo really didn't find anyone new?" he asks.

"There's only you," I promise. "Her human-mom found out about you two and banned her from the laundry room. But she never stopped loving you."

Rex gives me another slobbery lick. It's so rough, it sends me stumbling backward into Kaz. "She wants you to find a way to get to her," I add.

"A lover's path." Rex beams. "I guess it really is true what they say. Every dog has its day."

"Every dog has its day," I repeat. "I like that."

"The problem is, Marigold lives on the very top floor of this building." Rex's tail droops. "How am I supposed to reach her without getting caught?"

"The elevator?" Kaz offers.

Rex shakes his head. "Everyone in this building knows I live in the basement. I'll be stopped and returned to my human-dad before I make it to the second floor." He backs away and starts circling the room. "What I need is a path outside the building . . ." He pauses in front of a high window. A rusty metal contraption hangs outside. "The fire escape ladder," Rex says thoughtfully. "That could work." Rex lifts onto his hind legs to examine the window. "I'll need to find a time when my human-dad is out, of course . . ."

I interrupt before Rex can get too caught up in

planning. "Before we go," I say, "we were hoping you could help us."

Rex drops back down and turns around. He pulls back his lips, revealing his long, sharp teeth. I immediately tense. But this time, no snarl comes. Only a wide dog smile. "Anything for friends of my Maripoo," he beams.

I relax and sink onto my belly, resting my sore paws. "Marigold said you go to Central Park."

Rex nods. "Every Saturday."

"How do you get there?" I ask. "We're trying to get to Central Park ourselves."

"Easy." Rex sits back on his haunches. "My human-dad's brother drives a City Tours bus. It's a sightseeing bus," he explains. "One of the buses ends at Central Park, so he lets us ride it for free."

"Do you think Kaz and I could ride it?" I ask eagerly.

Rex studies me. "You're tiny enough to sneak on." He looks at Kaz. "And I've seen pigeons hitch a ride before. No one seems to care as long as they stay out of the way." He gives a gruff nod. "Yeah. You could probably get away with it."

Kaz looks interested. "How do we get there?"

"The stop is four blocks away. Follow the smell of flowers to the smell of paper to the smell of squirrels. You'll find it there. You want the northern side of the street," he adds.

"The nacho side?" I repeat. "Are there always nachos there?" My eyes flutter dreamily. I can almost taste the cheesy, crunchy goodness of rotten, hardened nachos. My stomach grumbles. It feels like a long time since I ate Marigold's treat.

"Not nacho," Rex corrects. "Northern."

My stomach grumbles more loudly. "So there are no nachos at all?"

"Ignore the rat," Kaz cuts in. "Northern side. Got it."

"Be sure you get on the bus that smells like leaves. That's how you'll know it ends in Central Park. Whatever you do, don't get on the bus that smells like rice. That one ends in Chinatown."

"Rice," I say dreamily. "With soy sauce."

"Focus, Raffie." Kaz hits me with his stubby wing. "Flowers, paper, squirrels," he repeats. "Northern corner. Leaf bus. Got it."

Rex wags his tail in approval. "Impressive."

"Pigeons are great at directions," I explain. "They've got brain compasses."

"Rex? Where are you, buddy?" A human voice rings out from the other side of the basement.

I stiffen. "Is that . . . ?"

"My human-dad," Rex confirms.

"The rat hater," I breathe.

"He doesn't like pigeons much either," Rex says. "You better go."

I dash to the stairs. But Kaz is limping. Slowly. He's still making his way across the room when a door slams on the other side of the basement. I peek out from the stairwell. A tall man is petting Rex. Everything about him is big. His hands. His head. His hair.

Come on, Kaz, I beg silently. Kaz limps faster. But he's not fast enough.

I can tell the moment the man sees him. His eyes pop. A vein bulges in his forehead. "How?" he gasps. "The exterminator was supposed to get rid of the pigeons!"

He reaches for something. It looks like a branch. A really thick, really hard branch. "Not the rat bat!" Rex howls.

The man takes no notice. "I have to do everything myself around here," he grumbles. He lifts the baseball bat and swings it at Kaz.

CHAPTER 20

Kill Two Birds with One Stone

Watch out, Kaz!" I scurry out from the stairwell and ram myself into Kaz. He tumbles onto his side. The bat misses him by a sliver.

"Are you kidding?" the man roars. "A rat too? I'm going to kill that exterminator. But first—" He lifts the bat above his head. "I'm going to kill you two."

The bat smashes down.

CRACK!

It just misses my tail.

CRACK!

The floor shakes under my paws.

The man storms toward us, swinging wildly. Kaz yelps as the bat slams down next to his hurt wing. I scurry backward, dashing left and right. Suddenly my tail bumps into something.

I turn around. I'm backed up against a wall.

"Got you." The man smiles. He lifts his bat.

"Stop!" Rex bounds toward his human-dad. "They're friends of my Maripoo." He leaps into the air. His front paws crash into his dad's chest. The man trips backward and falls to the ground. The bat falls with him. "Go!" Rex calls.

We hurry to the stairs. "You're not getting away," the man yells. I hear a scuffle behind us. The man is dragging himself across the floor, even with Rex's paws firmly planted on top of him. "What's gotten into you, Rex?" he grunts. He shrugs the dog off and clambers to his feet.

"Get through the door!" I tell Kaz.

We throw ourselves at the stairwell doorway. But the man reaches it first. The door slams shut in our faces.

Our exit is blocked. We're trapped.

The man lunges for his bat. "Don't do it," Rex whimpers, but his human-dad ignores his cries.

"Any ideas, Raffie?" Kaz asks shakily.

My whole body trembles. *Think*, I order myself. I remember my dad's three Ds. *Duck, dash, disappear.*

My eyes land on a vent in the bottom of the wall. It's small, but not so small that Kaz won't fit. The man lifts his bat into the air. "Now I've got you," he growls. "First, the rat." The bat whizzes toward me.

I leap desperately out of the way. "Over here," I gasp. I duck my head and dash to the vent. Then I squeeze through the slats to disappear. It's dark inside, but my whiskers automatically feel out the space. I give the vent a push. It falls off and lands on the ground with a clang. "Climb in," I tell Kaz. "Now!"

"Small spaces . . ." Kaz protests. Behind him, the man stomps toward us.

"Small spaces or a bat," I say. "Your choice."

The man closes the distance between us. His bat

zooms through the air. Kaz jumps into the vent with a squawk.

"I don't think so!" the man screams. "You are not getting away from me." He plunges the bat into the vent after us.

"Go!" I yell.

We turn and race through the darkness, into the space behind the wall.

CHAPTER 21

Bugging Out

My eyes glow in the darkness. I feel around with my whiskers. We're inside a large, steel pipe.

"Hate . . . small . . . spaces . . ." Kaz pants. We turn a corner. The vent is far behind us now. We're safe, at least from the bat. Kaz stops short and covers his head with his wings. His breath comes out in short, raspy bursts. "Gonna . . . get . . . stuck . . ."

"No, we're not," I promise. I look around. The pipe is wider than any I've ever been in. It's colder too. An icy breeze ruffles my fur. Behind me, I hear Kaz's beak start to chatter.

I scurry closer to Kaz. "I was always finding my way through pipes back home. I'll get us out of here, I promise."

Kaz doesn't lift his head. He looks so small all bunched up like that. It reminds me of the time Oggie

and I got lost in some pipes back home. He was so scared that he curled up in a ball and refused to move. I had to tell him twelve Raffie the Unstoppable stories to get him through those pipes. By the time we finally found our way home, my voice was hoarse and scratchy, but Oggie was beaming. "That was fun!" he cheered.

My stomach clenches at the memory. Wherever Oggie is now, I doubt there's anyone to tell him stories. I extract my claws. They scratch against steel. I have to get to Oggie. Which means I have to get Kaz moving.

"Come on, Kaz," I beg. "If you follow me, we'll be out of here soon." I take a long sniff. "I can smell the other end of the pipe. It's not that far away."

Kaz lifts his stubby wing and peers down the long

steel pipe. "Nah. Not happening." He shoves his head back under his wing.

"It's just a pipe, Kaz." I sigh. "What is it about small spaces that scares you so much?"

"I don't know." Kaz's head is still under his wing. His voice comes out all muffled. "I just hate 'em. Always have. A pigeon needs space to spread his wings."

"What if . . ." I think of Oggie. "What if I tell you a story while we walk?"

Kaz peeks out from under his wing. "Like the stories you tell your brother?"

I nod. "I've been told I'm the best storyteller there is." It's the truth. Oggie says that all the time.

Kaz shrugs his wings, then grunts in pain. "You can try."

I know exactly which story to tell. It's my new Raffie the Unstoppable story, the one I made up for Oggie's birthday. I get a stabbing feeling in my chest, like I accidentally swallowed a staple. I push it away and start talking.

"It was the best time in the subway station: before humans start their rush hour, but after the other rats have dragged their forages home behind the wall. Raffie the Unstoppable was alone on the subway platform, just the way he liked it. He was a lone adventurer in those days, a one-rat show. He was enjoying a relaxing forage along the platform when he heard a noise. It was a buzzing sound, a loud one. He turned and saw them. Bees. A whole swarm. They zoomed through the station. He could sense the very moment they saw him. Something in the air changed."

I can feel the story pumping through me, taking over. The pipe fades away. The cold air disappears. Suddenly I'm there, on the subway platform, the bees advancing toward me.

"They flew as a unit," I continue. "A single, angry, buzzing mass, swarming straight toward him. He could see their lethal stingers, dozens of them. The buzz was so loud he could barely hear himself think. All he knew was he had no way out."

I pull myself out of my storytelling daze and glance at Kaz. He's listening. I start inching forward down the pipe. He inches behind me.

"What happened next?" he asks. His breath isn't quite so raspy anymore. I scurry faster, and he matches my pace.

"The bees cornered Raffie the Unstoppable against the treasure chest," I continue. "They were so close, he could smell the venom in their stingers. So he did the only thing he could do. He prepared for battle."

"How?" Kaz breathes. The pipe bends left, then right. Kaz stays by my side.

"He extracted his claws. He flashed his incisors. He was going to go down, but not without a fight. The bees swarmed closer. One stinger skimmed his fur, then another. Suddenly, over the sound of buzzing, he heard a voice. 'Over here, bees!' it taunted. 'Come sting me instead!' Before Raffie the Unstoppable's very eyes, the bees backed away. Their buzzing grew more ferocious as they flew to their new victim."

"Who was it?" Kaz bursts out.

"It was a young rat, small and lithe. His name was Oggie the Brave. Oggie scurried down to the subway tracks. The bees zoomed after him. 'Let him be!' Raffie the Unstoppable yelled. He raced after the bees, calling them back, but it was too late. Oggie the Brave had caught their attention.

"They swarmed the subway tracks, their buzzing thunderous. Raffie the Unstoppable was shaking as he stopped at the edge of the platform. He knew what he'd find when he looked down. Oggie the Brave would have sacrificed himself for him.

"Except . . . the bees weren't stinging anyone. They were hovering in the air, their buzzes growing angrier and angrier with each passing second. And then he saw it. The pool of rainwater that had collected on the tracks the night before. Oggie the Brave was submerged beneath it, swimming furiously."

"Of course!" Kaz gasps as we continue down the pipe. The smell of fresh air gets stronger. The exit is close. "Bees won't go underwater."

"Exactly," I say. "They swarmed above, waiting for Oggie the Brave to reemerge. But Oggie knew those tracks like the back of his paw. He swam straight toward the electric third rail and stopped short—only a whisker's length away from it. The bees, however, had never heard of the third rail. They swarmed on top of it, waiting for Oggie to reemerge. Now, do you know how much electricity the subway track's third rail has? Six hundred and twenty-five volts. ZAP! ZAP! ZAP!" I yell. "One by one, that rail zapped the bees down, until not a single buzz rang through the air. Oggie the Brave had beaten the bees and saved the life of Raffie the Unstoppable." I pause and bow my head. "The. End."

"Whoa," Kaz breathes. "That story had me on the edge of my talons."

"I told you I'm a good storyteller," I boast. "And I can smell the exit to the pipe now. It's just over there."

Kaz picks up his pace at the promise of getting out of the pipe. "Those are some powerful stories you tell, Raffie."

I think of Oggie scurrying toward the slice of pizza on the subway platform. *Just like Raffie the Unstoppable!* he'd said. I look away, unable to meet Kaz's eyes. "Sure, they're good, but they're just stories," I mutter.

Kaz shakes his beak. "Just a story wouldn't have gotten me through this pipe."

We round a bend. The pipe narrows. Light streams

in, blinding us. "And now I'm outta here!" Kaz says. He pushes in front of me and hurries toward the light.

"Ow!" Kaz bumps into something. It stops him in his tracks. I skid to a stop behind him.

I blink into the light. Slowly, a shape emerges. It's a box with seven different entrances. They all lead down to a small, clear cage. I've seen one of these before, back home. "It's a bug trap," I say. "It's blocking our exit."

"Not good. Really not good." Kaz's feathers ruffle.

I press my nose to the clear plastic cage. Inside is a black bug. He's not moving. I shiver. "Poor guy. He never stood a chance."

The bug lifts his head.

I jump back with a yelp.

"My heavens," says the bug. "I do apologize if I frightened you."

My heart is still beating fast as I move closer to the trap. "I didn't realize you were alive," I say.

"Oh, yes. I was just taking a brief snooze." The bug crawls over to the window. He waves his antennae in a friendly gesture. "Salutations, good sirs," he says. "I do wonder if you could help me. It seems as if I've gotten myself into quite a jam."

CHAPTER 22

Free as a Bird

I'd tip my hat to you," the bug says. "But I seem to have lost it in my altercation with a water bug." His antennae stiffen. "Those insipid insects simply have no respect for the homes of others; wouldn't you agree?"

Kaz, who has been waddling in a frantic circle, searching for a way around the trap, pauses. "Uh . . . aren't *you* a water bug?"

The bug's mouth opens in a silent gasp. "My stars, no! I am of the strong and distinguished American cockroach species. I'm ashamed to admit that we do share some physical traits with the degenerates who go by the name of water bug, but I assure you, the similarities stop there." The bug pauses. "Oh dear, my apologies. Here I am pontificating on water bugs, yet I haven't formally introduced myself. I, my good sirs, am

Walter Sink." He dips his antennae low. "And who, may I ask, do I have the pleasure of encountering?"

"I'm Raffie Lipton," I say. I glance at Kaz. He's pacing again. He pauses only to peck at the edge of the trap. "And that's Kaz. He's . . . um . . . a little nervous. He hates small spaces."

"Hey," Kaz says in between pecks.

Walter waves hello with his antennae. "I must say, I'm quite pleased to make your acquaintances. I've been stuck here alone ever since that conniving water bug forced me into this trap. You see, first he goaded me with an insult about Elizabeth Toilet, our newly crowned queen. Then, when I turned to protect her good name, he cornered me against the northwest corner of the trap and—"

"Interesting," Kaz cuts in. He gives up on pecking and presses his beak against Walter's plastic cage. "But we're in a rush here." His breathing is growing raspier again. "Oggie's brother was rat-napped, and we've got to get to Central Park West to find him, which means we've got to get out of this building, which means we've got to get past your trap so we can GET OUT OF THIS PIPE!" The last words come out in a shout. Kaz's eyes dart wildly back and forth. "This very, very small pipe," he adds.

"That's quite a predicament you're in," Walter agrees. "I'm at your service to help. I would never dare stand in the way of such a noble quest." He looks down at his plastic trap. "Metaphorically speaking of course." He swishes his antennae thoughtfully. "Perhaps there is a mutually beneficial solution to this predicament."

I scrunch up my snout. "A what-huh?"

"What I mean to say is, if you could break apart this trap, you would have enough room to pass, while I would be freed. A favorable conclusion for all."

I bounce on my paws. "Like Lunch Box Chomp!"

"What?" Kaz grunts.

"It's a game I made up with Oggie. Human kids have

these little metal cupboards they carry around with them that are called lunch boxes. They're filled with food, and sometimes a kid will forget one on the subway platform. So Oggie and I came up with Lunch Box Chomp. The first one to gnaw open the lunch box wins."

I think of the last time I played with Oggie. Oggie won, because he's amazing at gnawing. He can gnaw a sneaker into a tunnel in three seconds flat. Inside the lunch box we found six perfectly rat-sized, perfectly aged pizza bagels. Oggie was so excited that he jumped on top of me, shouting, "Best game ever!"

A sob rises inside of me. I miss Oggie so much it hurts. It's ten times worse than my sore paws.

"You okay, Raffie?" Kaz pants.

I swallow hard. Missing Oggie isn't going to get me to him. But gnawing open Walter's trap will. "I'm fine." I straighten up and flash my incisors, showing them off. "Did I mention that rats are born gnawers?"

"Splendid," Walter says.

"So you gonna gnaw open this trap or what?" Kaz asks.

"Going to," I correct automatically. Kaz ignores me and gives the plastic another peck.

"Please." Walter gestures at his cage with his antennae. "Be my guest."

I examine the trap, searching for where the plastic is thinnest. Lulu taught me that trick when I first learned to gnaw. A section in the corner is slightly worn. Perfect. I crouch down low and begin to chew.

Walter watches me work. "You really are quite skilled," he says.

"You should see my little brother," I say between bites.

"Can you gnaw through anything?" Walter asks.

"Pretty much. Except for really thick steel. That's what rattraps and cages are made of." Just thinking of Oggie's cage makes me angry. I gnaw faster. Harder. A crack grows in the trap. Before long, there's a crumbling sound, and the whole thing collapses to pieces.

"Finally," Kaz breathes. "Let's ditch this pipe."

Walter crawls delicately out of the crumbled cage. "I couldn't have said it better myself."

CHAPTER 23

Queen Bee

"Freedom!" Kaz races toward the vent at the end of the pipe. Light streams in through it. A voice, too.

"Good evening, Mr. Howard . . . Going out for a late dinner, Miss Smith?"

I recognize that voice. It belongs to Sal the doorman. We're right back where we started, at the lobby. I groan. "Not the exit I was hoping for."

"Who cares?" Kaz rams his beak into the vent. It rattles, but doesn't dislodge. "Let's get out of here."

"And then what?" I argue. "Your wing's bruised, remember? You can't fly. And I've seen how fast you waddle."

"If you prefer an alternate exit, you could accompany me home," Walter offers. "There is a vent near our burrow that should be quite easy to depart through. It's close to the sidewalk."

"There are no doormen there?" I ask. "Or rat-hating supers?"

"I should hope not." Walter's antennae shudder. "Besides, I'm sure our queen will be eager to show her appreciation for my safe return. Perhaps she'll be able to proffer assistance with your quest."

"And just how far away is this burrow?" Kaz asks.

"It's right down the golden highway." Walter points an antenna at a brass pipe that winds along next to the vent. "Then we'll cross the silver bridge and reach our burrow behind the sink."

"We're in," I say.

Kaz takes a deep breath. "Okay," he agrees.

We follow Walter onto the brass pipe. I scurry after him easily, but Kaz has to duck his head to fit. The pipe winds through the wall, past globs of dust and sheets of insulation and wafts of mustiness. I breathe in the familiar, homey scents. "Here's the silver bridge," Walter calls back. It's a cinder block. On the other side is a wide patch of ground covered in a thin coat of water. The whole place is crawling with Walter lookalikes.

"Welcome to the burrow," Walter says grandly. "I assure you that our puddle is of the oldest, moldiest quality. We're quite fortunate that the leak in apartment 1C's sink has gone undetected for years."

Before Walter can say more, a young cockroach sidles

up to him. "King Walter!" he squeals. "You've returned to us! Mother, the king is home!"

All at once, the activity in the burrow comes to a sudden stop. At least a dozen bugs turn in Walter's direction. "All hail the king!" someone cries. Suddenly they all lower their antennae in matching bows.

"King?" Kaz repeats.

"Oh, did I not mention that?" Walter asks calmly.

My eyes pop as I take in the bowing bugs. "You mentioned the new queen," I say.

"That," Walter says proudly, "would be my lovely new wife. Speaking of . . ."

A broad, stately cockroach crawls over. She's a lighter color than Walter, and she swishes her antennae gracefully as she approaches. Resting on her head is a wreath of bristles. "Walter?" Her voice is high and strong. "Is that really you, darling? I thought you were . . . I was so scared . . ." The rest of her words are lost in a sob.

"I'm home, my love." Walter wraps his antennae around her. "Thanks to these brave gentlemen."

The queen turns her attention to Kaz and me. "You have brought our king back to us. We cockroaches believe no good deed shall go unpaid. Please, tell me what I can do for you in return."

"They are venturing northward, to search for Raffie's brother, who's been cruelly rat-napped," Walter says.

"Do you have anything that might assist them on such a noble quest?"

The queen is quiet for a moment, thinking. "I believe I have just the thing. Follow me."

She leads us along a wet path. As we pass, each cockroach respectfully lowers his or her antennae, murmuring in a low voice.

"Are they bowing to you?" I ask.

"Not this time," the queen replies. "They're bowing to you. Listen."

I cock an ear, and soon I'm able to make out what the bugs are murmuring. "All hail the heroes."

"Heroes," I whisper. I give my whiskers a twitch. "Hear that, Kaz?"

"Oh yeah." Kaz fluffs his feathers. "I could get used to this."

"Here we are." The queen stops in front of a shiny pink box. "This," she explains, "is where we store our most valuable acquisitions." The queen crawls up the side of the box and flicks the clasp with an antenna. She noses the top open. Immediately, music begins to twinkle, and a small plastic girl in a pouffy dress spins round and round.

"A jewelry box," Kaz says. "I've seen those in windows before."

I peek into the box. Inside lies a collection of forages. There are bottle caps and buttons and fork heads and toothpicks and a fluffy yellow rectangle that reeks of soap.

"We're a pacifist community," the queen assures us. "But if the water bugs ever initiate attack, we must be ready." She crawls into the box. There's some light clinging and clanging as items are shuffled about.

Finally, the queen reemerges. She's carrying a small white oval in her antennae. "Walter acquired this during his travels. It's a magic bean, consumed by Mr. Turner in apartment 6B every night. According to Walter, it contains the power to make a grown human fall asleep."

"A sleeping pill," Kaz offers.

"Call it what you will," the queen says. "All I know is it's quite powerful. I've been saving it to use on the water bug king, in case of emergency." She crawls out of the box and secures the top. "But instead I bestow it upon you as a token of our sincerest appreciation." She passes the white oval to Kaz. "Please, use it wisely."

Kaz tucks the oval safely under a feather. "Thanks," he says.

Walter crawls over, and a long line of bugs follows closely behind. "Pardon my delay. The others don't seem to want to let me out of their sight."

"Your queen gave us a magic bean," I tell him.

"Sleeping pill," Kaz corrects.

"Ah, I'm glad," Walter says. "My queen has the most astute of instincts. I do hope it will be of service to you. Speaking of which, you must want to be on your way." He leads us to a wooden beam.

"Best of luck," the queen calls out behind us.

"All hail the heroes!" the other bugs chant.

I give a wave with my tail and slip under the beam. On the other side is a tall, smooth wall. In the center is a vent. "It leads directly to the street," Walter says.

"*Street* . . . I've never been happier to hear that word in my life," Kaz replies.

"Thank you," I say to Walter.

"Best of luck, good sirs." Walter dips his antennae in a bow. Then he slips back under the beam and disappears. I scurry up to the vent and push it off with my paws. Fresh night air rushes in, smelling of leaves and cars.

I bow to Kaz, in an imitation of Walter. "After you, good sir."

TRUST FUND DOG FINDS LOVE

MARIGOLD ROSE VALENCIA THE THIRD, the beloved star of the reality TV show *Trust Fund Dog*, has done it all. She's won Best in Show at the Westminster Kennel Club Dog Show. She's flown in a helicopter over the Maldives. She's done a photo shoot at the top of Paris's Eiffel Tower. She's even been the face of a political campaign, poodles for the president. There's only one thing Marigold Rose Valencia the Third hasn't conquered, and that's love.

Until now.

On tonight's episode of *Trust Fund Dog*, Marigold and her owner, Lady Wilma Harris, suffered a shock when a large dog named Rex climbed off the fire escape and right through the window of their apartment. Film footage captured by passersby down below showed the dog accomplishing an unheard of feat: climbing a fire-escape ladder for thirty-two floors in order to reach Marigold's penthouse apartment.

At the sight of this intruder—a part pitbull, part mastiff wearing a spiked collar—Lady Harris screamed in terror. But Marigold galloped straight toward Rex, and viewers of the show were treated to one of the most joyous reunions ever to be featured on reality TV. A video of Marigold leaping into Rex's paws has already been viewed over a million times, earning Marigold's untraditional suitor the nickname "mutt in shining armor."

Lady Harris has released the following statement regarding the dogs' relationship. "I admit I was originally reluctant to give my blessing, given Rex's mixed pedigree. But it has become clear to me that this dog would do anything for my Marigold—even scale the tallest building—and what more could a mother ask for? I wish them both nothing but happiness together."

A new reality show is already rumored to be in the works, featuring Marigold and Rex. It will be called *Beauty and the Mutt.*

CHAPTER 24

Squirrel Away

W e've got to follow the smell of flowers to the smell of paper to the smell of squirrels," Kaz says. "Those were Rex's directions. This is all you, Raffie. Smells are rat territory."

I scurry into a shadow on the dark street and take a sniff. Immediately I catch the disgustingly sweet stench of flowers. "This way." Kaz waddles along next to me. He moves more slowly than usual, thanks to his bruised wing. I slow my pace to match his.

We find the flowers in a gated patch of green. A streetlamp glows nearby, illuminating their petals. There are so many that I nearly throw up. "What is this horrible place?" I groan.

"It's called a garden," Kaz says. "Humans think they're pretty."

"Pretty *gross*." I gag. "Let's get out of here before I pass out from the stench."

I take a quick, deep sniff. Under that awful, no-good flower stench, I catch a whiff of something better. It smells like MetroCards and balled-up receipts. It smells like soggy napkins and old newspaper. It reminds me so much of home that my heart must be turning into pizza, because it feels like someone's gobbling it right up.

I lead Kaz toward the smell. It takes us to a large blue box. "A mailbox," Kaz says. I take a whiff. If I close my eyes, I can almost believe I'm in the sorting nook, on paper duty with Oggie. I remember one of the last things we sorted: that sheet of stickers. Lulu put an *I* ♥ *NY* sticker on Oggie's ear, and even though he hated it, he did look cute. I wonder if somewhere in 220 Central Park West that sticker is still on his ear.

I take another sniff. "Squirrels," I announce. "This way."

"I hate squirrels," Kaz mutters as he follows me toward the smell. "They're some nasty hoarders."

"I've never really met one," I reply. "Every once in a while, a squirrel will wander down to the station by mistake, but they never stick around long enough to talk."

"That's 'cause they're greedy little devils," Kaz says.

"They don't stick around unless you have something they want."

"Like acorns?" I ask.

"Nah. They get acorns, no problem. What squirrels really want is shiny stuff to squirrel away. Coins, gems, beads, rings—that's the stuff they live for. Once, this building I was perching on had a theft problem. Jewelry kept disappearing from apartments. The cops would come and say all these theories. It was the doorman; it was the super; it was the man in apartment 8D. Then one day, I fly up to the roof and you know what I find? One of the bricks on the ledge is hollow, and it's filled with jewelry. And guess who's sleeping next to it? A squirrel. The building didn't have a thief. It had a *squirrel*."

"I heard a human call a squirrel a tree rat once," I say.

Kaz shakes his beak. "Believe me, you're nothing like a squirrel. They'll do anything—sink to any level—for something shiny."

It doesn't take us long to find the source of the squirrel smell. It's a tall tree. I look up. A wide, bushy tail flicks out of sight. I curl my own tail in my paws. Kaz is right. That gross, fluffy tail is nothing like mine.

"See that hole up in the tree?" Kaz whispers. I look up. I spot a round, hollow hole in the tree bark. "That's called a knot. I bet it's filled with squirrel loot. Word is that every tree in the city has some squirrel plunder stashed away in it."

I watch as a squirrel dashes along a narrow branch and disappears into the leaves. A second later he's back. He's holding something small and hard between his paws. "What's that?" I ask Kaz. Or I mean to. But halfway through the question, something hits me in the snout.

"Ow! What in the name of trash was that?"

Something hits me again. And again. They're acorns. Another one bounces off my back. "Hey!" I shout. "Stop that!"

There's no answer. Just a low, deep laugh. Another acorn smacks into my head. Kaz pushes me under a bush. "What did I tell you? They're nasty little devils. But look. That's the northern side of the street, like Rex said." Kaz points his stubby wing at a sign on the street corner. "I wonder what that says."

"City Tours," I read slowly. "It's the bus stop!" There's another line on the bottom of the sign. It takes me a while, but finally I read, *"Tours from 8–8 daily."*

Kaz looks at the sky. It's pitch black. The only light comes from street lamps and the windows of buildings.

"I hate to tell you this, but it's definitely after eight." Kaz lies down under the bush and adjusts his bruised wing. "Looks like we're spending the night."

"No. No way." I pace in a circle around Kaz. "We can't waste a whole night *sleeping*! Oggie is lost. Who knows what could happen by morning? What if the E word comes? What if we're too late?" I nudge Kaz with my snout. "We have to keep going."

Kaz closes his eyes. He cocks his head. He spreads out his nonbruised wing and flexes his talons.

"What are you doing?" I ask impatiently.

"I'm listening to my brain compass." The green feathers on his neck ruffle. He opens his eyes. "I can *feel* Central Park, Raffie, deep in my feathers. And let me tell you: it's not close. Not even a little bit." He shakes his beak. "I want to get to Central Park just as badly as you. You know I do. But we need that bus to get there." I open my snout to argue, but Kaz cuts me off. "We'll take the first bus in the morning," he says. "I'm telling you. This is the fastest way."

I close my snout. I know he's right. But all I can think about is Oggie, spending the night alone in a cage. He needs me, and here I am, resting under a bush, like I don't have a care in the world. I fight back a yawn. "I can't just go to sleep with Oggie in trouble," I say.

Kaz's head droops sleepily toward his wing. He forces it back up. "Then we won't sleep," he says. "We'll . . . make a plan."

"A plan could be good," I say reluctantly. I rest my snout on my paws. "And we could get a lot of planning done in a full night." The thought cheers me up, just a little. "Okay. By the time that bus comes, we'll be ready for anything."

CHAPTER 25

Make a Beeline for It

Wake up! Raffie! I want to be the first ones out there!"

I open one eye. Oggie is running in circles around my shoe box. "It's Ratmas!" he cheers.

I pop up. It's here. The best day of the year. "Okay, here's our game plan," I tell Oggie as I hop out of bed. "You'll take the front of the treasure chest, and I'll take the back." I grab a small white carton in my teeth. I foraged it yesterday and licked it clean of sticky rice. Soon, it will be filled with delicious, sugary treats.

"Tell me the story of Ratmas again, Raffie," Oggie begs.

"A long time ago, there was a very special human," I tell him as we scurry out into the station. "His name was Halloween. Halloween decided that, for one day

*of the year, humans and rats should call a truce. On
this day, humans wouldn't hate rats—instead, they'd
honor them. Now, Ratmas comes once a year, on the
first of November. On this beautiful day, humans fill
our treasure chests with candy wrappers still smudged
with chocolate and boxes of candy that are still half-
full, and every once in a while—"*

"A whole, uneaten candy bar," Oggie breathes.

"It's the best day of the year," I finish.

*We scurry side by side up the treasure chest. It's
filled with so many wrappers I don't know where to
begin.*

Oggie's whiskers twitch with excitement. "Happy Ratmas, Raffie."

"Raffie. Raffie!"

"Happy Ratmas," I whisper.

"Hey, wake up. You're talking in your sleep."

I open one eye, then the other. There's a wing on my back, shaking me. My heart drops all the way to my paws. It's Kaz, not Oggie.

"What's Ratmas?" Kaz asks.

"It's Oggie's and my favorite day," I say with a yawn. I blink in the bright light. I've seen the sun before, of course: glowing, golden rays that slide down the subway station stairs. I've even seen it outside, just before night takes charge and sends it away. But I've never seen it like this. It's hot and bright and fiery, and it lights me up like I'm standing under the headlights of a train.

I bolt upright. "Kaz, we must have fallen asleep while we were planning! It's already morning time! We have to get to Oggie."

"No problem, because look at me." Kaz lifts into the air and flies in a lopsided circle.

"Your bruised wing is working again!" I exclaim. I flex my paws. They're not so sore anymore either. I think of the plan we came up with last night, before we apparently fell asleep. It just might work.

"Kaz! Look!" A huge, red bus is driving down the

street. It has two floors. The top floor is open: no ceilings, no walls.

"A double-decker," Kaz says.

The bus slows to a stop next to the City Tours sign. "All aboard!" a cheerful voice booms. "See Times Square! The Empire State Building! Central Park! Hop on and off as you please!"

I leap to my paws. The smell of leaves pours off the bus, just like Rex described. "This is the one!" I say. "This will take us to Oggie!"

"And Central Park," Kaz says dreamily. He swoops down next to me. "You ready for our plan?"

I nod. I have to get all the way across the street and onto that bus without being seen. "Let's do it."

Kaz flies low to the ground. I crouch under his wings as I scurry along the sidewalk. His feathers drape over me, hiding me from sight. "Here comes the hard part," Kaz murmurs. "Ready. Set. Stairs!"

I scurry as fast as I can. Up and up and up. Kaz flies on top of me. His wings bump my head and my back, but I keep going. Voices drift down.

"Mira la paloma!"

"Is the pigeon visiting New York too, Mommy?"

I block the voices out. I have to focus. Up and up. Higher and higher. Finally, I hop up the last stair. We're on the top floor of the bus. Wind ripples through my fur. The sun burns down on my tail. I dart under a seat before anyone can see me. Kaz lands on top of the seat. "We made it," he pants.

I wait a minute before peeking out. A clump of humans is gathered at the back of the bus. A kid points at Kaz and waves, but, as usual, no one else pays him any attention. I feel a pang of jealousy, but I quickly push it away. I only have room for one thing in my brain right now, and that's getting to Central Park West.

"Oggie, here we come," I whisper.

"Welcome to the Big Apple!" The booming voice is back. It pours out through a black box at the front of the bus. "This is the melting pot, the city that never sleeps, some say, the capital of the world. We're in New York City, and there's no place quite like it. So sit back and enjoy the ride!"

CHAPTER

Can't Squirrel out of This

The bus bumps and rattles as it winds through the city streets. We've been driving for a while when Kaz squeezes under the seat with me. "I've got some bad news," he says. His head bobs as he peeks out from under the seat. From this low down, all I can see are the tips of buildings, poking at the sky like toothpicks. It reminds me of the time Oggie and I built a miniature Brooklyn out of forages. We used toothpicks and popsicle sticks for the buildings because Oggie insisted they looked most accurate. I swallow hard. I would give anything to be able to scurry to him right now and tell him he was right. "What is it, Kaz?" I ask.

Kaz's eyes meet mine. They have a nervous, flickery look to them. "My brain compass is telling me we're going *away* from Central Park."

"No." My voice comes out a little too loudly, and I hastily lower it. "That's not possible. We got on the bus that smells like leaves. Just like Rex said. This has to be it. It has to be! My nose never steers me wrong."

"Neither does my brain compass," Kaz says. "And it's sending me all kinds of *wrong way* signals." He flaps up into the air for a better look. "Not good," he mutters. "Really not good." He lowers back down next to me. "I can see the Brooklyn Bridge again, Raffie. We're right back where we started."

"No, no, no." My tail tenses up in a tight curl. "This can't be happening. We already wasted a whole night sleeping, and now we're back where we started? How are we ever going to get to Oggie?" Panic clutches at my chest, making it hard to breathe. "We have to get off," I pant. "We have to find another way. We have to—"

"Wait." Kaz holds up a wing. "The bus is talking again."

"Soon we will be reaching Battery Park," the cheerful voice booms. "As your guidebook explains, City Tours has started taking this nontraditional path through the city because we believe that no trip to Manhattan is complete without a view of one of our most meaningful monuments, the Statue of Liberty."

"Who cares about some statue, whatever that is," I hiss. "We've got to get off this bus, Kaz."

Kaz cocks his head. "Hold on."

"After this," the voice continues, "we will begin our regular drive uptown, ending at the world-famous Central Park."

Kaz gives his wings an excited flutter. "False alarm," he breathes. "Looks like we're just taking a little detour."

I collapse on the floor, panting with relief. "As we pull up to Battery Park," the booming voice continues, "let me tell you a little about the Statue of Liberty. When a ship sails into the New York Harbor, the Statue of Liberty is one of the first things its passengers see. You might notice the tablet she's holding. It's inscribed with the date of the American Declaration of Independence: July 4, 1776. You might also notice the broken chain lying at her feet, and the lit torch she holds. To those arriving in New York, the Statue of Liberty is a symbol of the greatest gift of all. Freedom."

The bus screeches to a stop. "I want to go down to the water, Daddy!" a boy says from somewhere behind us.

"All right, y'all," a man replies. "Looks like we're hopping off." Feet pound past us, one after another. They climb down the stairs and fade into the distance. I poke my head out from under the seat. There's no one left. We're all alone on the top floor of the bus.

Kaz flies straight to the ledge of the bus. "Come look at this view, Raffie!" he calls out.

I glance around. There are no humans to see me. I can do whatever I want. I scamper up onto the ledge, next to Kaz. The sun warms my back. A sparrow hops around down below. From this high up, he looks teeny tiny.

"There's the Statue of Liberty," Kaz says. I follow his gaze across the water to something standing in the distance. It looks like a human, but it's taller, and straighter, and stiller. The statue-human holds one arm up in the air. "I used to watch her back home in Brooklyn," Kaz says. "I'd escape from my flock for a few minutes and stare at her across the water, imagining what it would be like to just take off and fly to her—to be free from it all." Kaz pauses. "And now I am," he says slowly. He lifts his wing into the air, just like the statue's arm. "The Kaz of Liberty!" he shouts.

I laugh, but inside I feel all jittery. Kaz might be free, but Oggie isn't. And every second we're here is another second he's trapped in that cage. Or worse.

"Off we go!" The bus's booming voice is back. I hear a shuffle of feet below, but not a single human climbs to the top of the bus. I blow out a sigh of relief and relax on the ledge. "Welcome to the Big Apple! We're going to cruise our way uptown, ending at Central Park. Next stop, Union Square!" The bus lurches forward. I have to dig my claws into the ledge to keep from tumbling off. But then we're moving, and it's nothing like riding the subway.

Wind whips through my fur and whooshes in my ears. Smells race past, one after another, so fast I barely have time to sniff them before they're gone. The voice keeps booming out of the black box, but I've stopped listening. There are too many other sounds blasting on every side of us: honks and sirens and voices and music.

We move faster. Buildings stretch toward the sky, shiny as tinfoil. Lights flash: green, yellow, red. Sidewalks unspool like thread, and humans hurry down them. For a second I worry a woman spots me, but then she's gone, and it doesn't matter.

"This is Union Square!" the voice booms. The streets are crowded here, filled with cars and humans and lined with windows. One window is packed with clothes. Human-sized dolls pose stiffly inside it. They make me think of the doll Mom made Lulu once out of a cotton ball and Twizzlers. "My sister would love this place," I murmur.

And then we're moving again, the wind whistling in my ears. We pass fountains and patches of green; we pass signs that seem to float in midair; we pass more windows filled with clothes and windows filled with food. One window is filled only with cheese, and my stomach rumbles with a reminder that I've never in my life gone this long without eating.

Soon, the bus slows down again. "Here we are at our next stop: the Empire State Building," the booming voice announces. "This skyscraper stands one hundred and two stories tall!"

I look up. The building towers above all the others. A needle juts out from the top of it, stabbing the sky. It's the biggest thing I've ever seen. I feel itsy-bitsy beneath it, smaller than an ant. Down below, I spot a human eating a muffin, and my stomach lets out a hungry roar. Kaz laughs. "You better do something about that before your stomach gives us away."

I scurry off the ledge and start sniffing around for food. I find half a sandwich wedged under a seat. It's nice and slimy, just the way I like it. I gobble part of it up and bring the rest to Kaz. "It's no grass seeds, but I'll take what I can get," Kaz says.

"Not on my bus, you won't, darling."

I whip around. A squirrel is standing at the top of the bus's stairs. His voice is low and breathy. He glitters in the sun, and as he glides over to us, I see why. The squirrel is dripping in diamonds. A diamond watch is belted around his stomach. A diamond necklace is twisted up his tail. Diamond rings glitter around each of his paws. "This bus, and all of its fabulous spoils, belongs to me. So just give that divine little sandwich

to Sparkle here and get off the bus, and no one will get hurt."

Kaz bursts out laughing. "Get a load of this guy." He pecks hungrily at the sandwich. "Like some squirrel could kick us off the bus."

"Yeah," I agree loudly. It comes out a little shaky, though. The squirrel might be the same size as Kaz, but he's a lot bigger than me.

"Oh, sweetie," the squirrel says in his breathy voice. "You're not from around here, are you? Otherwise, you would know I'm not *some squirrel.*" The squirrel swishes his tail. His diamonds glimmer and clink. "I'm Sparkle the Sassy Squirrel, and I'm more famous than you can *imagine.* Last I heard, I have five hundred and sixteen YouTube features."

"Whoa!" I exclaim. "What kind of tubes are those?" Sparkle the Squirrel gives me a weird look, and I shake my snout. It doesn't matter anyway. Rubber tubes, plastic tubes, paper tubes—any of them would make a killer tunnel if you had five hundred and sixteen.

Sparkle climbs up next to us. "I have thousands of adoring fans. And do you know why? Because I give the tourists what they want. Glamour. Excitement. A taste of the New York City high life. And when they switch from fawning over me to admiring the photos they took of me, I slip into their shopping bags, and I do some shopping of my own." He tosses back his head to show off a chain of diamonds looped around his neck. "The bus's next stop is in the Diamond District. That, honey, is where the magic happens. If you're not off the bus by then, I'll have to make you get off."

Now even I'm laughing. "Make us? How?"

Kaz looks up from the sandwich. "There's two of us and only one of you," he points out.

"Oh, to be so deliciously innocent." Sparkle shakes

his head. His gems wink in the sunlight. "I'm going to tell you one more time. This is my bus. And I want you off."

"No." The word slips right out of my snout. I can't help it. I'm finally getting close to Oggie. I can't let anyone stop me now. "I'm getting to my brother," I insist.

Sparkle glides closer, until we're snout to snout. His breath smells like mint. "Let's try that again, sweetie." His black, beady eyes lock with mine. He doesn't blink. "I said, I want you off."

My breath catches in my chest, but I don't back down. "And I said no," I repeat. "This bus is going to Central Park, and so are we. Nothing is getting in our way." My snout curls up, revealing my incisors.

Sparkle flicks his glittery tail. "We'll just have to see about that," he says.

The bus rumbles. Footsteps pound onto the first floor. The booming voice returns. "Welcome to the Big Apple!"

"Do you hear that voice, darling?" Sparkle asks. "That voice belongs to the driver, Carlos. He's my most adoring fan. When I come aboard, Carlos's tips triple. He would do anything for me."

The bus pulls into the street. Sparkle turns away from us. Slowly, he climbs along the ledge, toward the front of the bus. Buildings swirl past. Wind blows back my whiskers. The booming voice keeps talking as the bus picks up speed. Sparkle stops at the front of the bus. He crouches down on the ledge and looks back over his shoulder. "Don't say I didn't warn you," he calls out. Then he jumps off the bus.

For a second, I can see him in the air: legs splayed out, tail ruffling, diamonds sparkling. He gives us a wink, and then he plummets to the street.

The booming voice is replaced by a gasp. "What in the—no! SPARKLE!"

The bus lurches. It shrieks. It jerks to a sudden, short stop.

I can't hold on tight enough. I fly off the ledge and tumble through the air. The world spins around me: ground, sky, ground, sky. And then I'm plunging down and it's only ground, ground, ground.

I catch a glimpse of Sparkle landing gracefully on all fours. *He planned this*, I realize. Then I smash into the sidewalk, and everything goes black.

 Publishers Daily

FAMOUS SQUIRREL NABS PICTURE BOOK SERIES

A NEW YORK CITY institution in his own right, Sparkle the Sassy Squirrel has the stats of a star. He's been featured on YouTube over five hundred times, and his videos surpass eight million in views. His photograph has been published in *New York Magazine*, *Time Out New York*, and multiple guidebooks. Now Sparkle will add another credential to his already impressive resume.

The diamond-loving squirrel will be featured in a new picture book series by famed children's book author Tommy Rivers. The first book, *Sparkle Takes Manhattan*, is slated for publication in the summer and already has thousands of preorders.

Following the announcement, Tommy Rivers went on *The Today Show* to discuss his new project. "I live near 47th Street's Diamond District, so I've personally encountered Sparkle several times," he said. "For me, Sparkle is one of the reasons that New York is such a unique city. Only in New York can you find a diamond-wearing squirrel showing off for tourists! I'm honored to bring Sparkle and his sassy New Yorker attitude to kids all over the world."

CHAPTER

In the Lion's Den

Ow.

Ow ow ow ow.

My head feels like a wad of gum on the subway platform: smashed and mashed all out of shape. Black spots swim in my vision. Everything looks fuzzy: my paws, the bowl of water next to me, the metal bars—

BARS?

I blink furiously. My head roars with pain, but slowly my vision clears.

Bars. Thick steel bars. On every side of me.

I'm inside a cage.

My heart pounds harder than my head. This can't be happening. I squeeze my eyes shut. I think of the last thing I remember. Sparkle the Squirrel . . . getting tossed from the bus . . . and then . . . nothing. I must have gotten knocked out. Which means this is a dream. I'll open my eyes again and it will all be gone.

I open my eyes.

I still see bars.

"Well, look. The sweet little sugar pie is coming to."

I tense. I'm not alone. Slowly, I inch forward. I peek through the bars of my cage. "Whoa," I whisper.

I'm inside a room. It's lined with shelves, and on those shelves are several cages, and in those cages are animals. My eyes dart wildly from one to another. Raccoon. Possum. Cat.

My vision goes fuzzy again. I sway on my paws. Why am I in the same room as a *cat*?

A plump skunk lifts a glossy black paw in a wave. A thick white line runs down her back and along her tail. "Well, aren't you precious," she drawls.

"Poor kid." This comes from the possum. He's long and gray, his fur streaked white with age. "He looks terrified."

"'Course he's terrified, Pierre," the raccoon snaps. "Look at where we are."

"Where?" I whisper. "Where are we?"

The cat snorts. "Shocking that a dim-headed rat wouldn't know." His voice is sharp and scratchy, like claws scraping against subway tracks. I shiver. It almost makes me glad for the bars that separate us.

"Sure, Slink," says a shrill voice. I look down to find another rat in a cage beneath the raccoon. She's long

and lean and has several patches of fur missing. "If only we could all be as brilliant as the cat who got caught pilfering milk from the mayor's home."

Slink the cat's tail bristles. "Say what you will, Truella, but like I said, this rat clearly doesn't know."

"Know what?" I ask desperately. I gnash at the bars of my cage, but they're made of thick steel. I can't gnaw through them. I can't squeeze through them, either. The gaps between the bars are too narrow. This cage is built for a rat.

Pierre the possum yawns, revealing old, yellowed teeth. "I hate to be the bearer of bad news, kid, but we're in Animal Control."

"No." I slide down to my belly. All I know about Animal Control is that once you go in, you never come out.

"Poor little peach," the skunk coos. "It could be worse. We're not in the bad room." She shivers, making her white stripe ruffle. "That's where they take the sick and crazy ones. This room here is just the nuisance room."

"I knocked over one too many trash cans," the raccoon grumbles.

"I made it here all the way from Savannah, Georgia, just to spray the wrong human," the skunk says with a sigh.

"I played possum for a minute too long," Pierre adds.

"And I hear that you fell off the top of a bus," the skunk says. "Got yourself knocked out cold. And bless your heart, you got lucky, too. From what I've heard, Animal Control would normally have finished a rat off right then and there—"

"A travesty," scoffs Truella the rat.

The skunk shrugs her tail. "Maybe so, Truella, but you know it's true. But apparently there was a huge crowd around you and the pigeon, and Animal Control didn't want that kind of publicity. So they shipped you off to us instead."

"How long have I been in here?" My voice comes out all raspy. I'm finding it hard to breathe.

"You were out for the whole night," the skunk offers.

"What? That's too long!" I ram myself into the bars of the cage. "I have to get out of here." I claw and gnash. My head throbs, but I don't care. Pain doesn't matter anymore. All that matters is getting free. "My brother needs me. And I have to find Kaz!"

"Is that the pigeon?" Pierre asks with a yawn.

I nod. "He was helping me find my brother. He was tossed off the bus too, and he could be hurt. He already has one wing that's—"

"Stubby?" the raccoon offers.

"Yes." My head snaps up. "How did you know?"

"Psychic," he grunts.

"Oh, don't you get too big for your britches on us, Rory," the skunk scolds. "Honey pie, there's a pigeon in the cage next to yours. He's got one stubby wing, and he's been sleeping ever since you two got here."

"Kaz!" I jam the tip of my snout through the bars. Out of the corner of my eye, I can just make out one of Kaz's talons. "Kaz! Wake up!"

"Raffie? That you?" Kaz's voice is groggy. I hear the rustling of feathers. His beak pokes through the bars of his cage. "I'm in a small space." Panic creeps into his voice. "This is not good. Really not good."

"Okay, stay calm," I say quickly, even though I'm anything but. "We're in Animal Control, but we're just in the nuisance room. So we can find a way out, right?"

"Sure," Rory the raccoon grumbles. "In your dreams."

"I'm fixin' to spray you right about now, Rory," the skunk says.

"You're all talk, Sabrina," Rory scoffs. "You know that spraying will get you sent to 3C."

"We're all going there one day anyway," Sabrina says. "I might as well get a good spray in first."

"What's 3C?" I ask.

"Room 3C," Rory grunts. "Also known as the last place you'll ever see."

A cry escapes me.

"Not good," Kaz whispers. "Really really not good."

"Don't worry," Sabrina says soothingly. "Just think of it as beddy-bye. A nice, long nap."

"Yeah," Rory snorts. "Really long."

"But I can't nap!" I say. "I have to get to Central Park West. I have to save my brother."

The door to the room swings open. The animals all fall silent. A man walks in. He's short and thin and has so much hair, it looks like a bird's nest. He slumps down at the table in the corner of the room and drops a key next to him. He's carrying what smells like an egg sandwich and a soda, but for once, my stomach doesn't even grumble.

"Jimmy?" Another man pokes his head into the room. "Why are you eating in here?"

"I just want one breakfast without Mary breathing down my neck," Jimmy groans.

The other man nods. "I hear you. Well, take your time. But when you're done, Mary says she wants this room cleared."

Jimmy's eyes widen. *"Cleared?"*

The other man shrugs. "That's what she said. Something about wanting to take advantage of the publicity when those photos of the rat and pigeon hit the Internet." He looks around the room with a sigh. "Seems extreme to me, but she's the boss."

"And she never lets us forget it." Jimmy takes a sip of soda. "I'll start the transports to 3C after I eat."

The air in the room is suddenly much too thick. "Did he just say . . . ?" I'm shaking too much to finish the sentence.

Pierre's old, tired eyes meet mine. "'Fraid so, kid."

In the next cage over, Rory glares at me. "Thanks to you, sounds like we're all going to 3C."

CHAPTER 28

Nervous as a Long-Tailed Cat in a Room Full of Rocking Chairs

My legs wobble like congealed jelly. I gasp for a breath, but I can't seem to draw any in. Images flash through my mind. Oggie, climbing into my shoe box at night. Oggie, sliding down a slop-and-slide I made him out of leftover slop. Oggie, trapped in a cage, terrified and alone.

I collapse onto my belly. I can't believe this is happening. Oggie will never get home. I'll never see my family again. And all these animals . . . My eyes dart from cage to cage. They're all going to 3C. I bury my head in my paws. "I'm so sorry," I whisper into my fur.

"Don't feel bad, sugar pie," Sabrina says. "We were all going there eventually."

"Yeah, but not today," Slink grumbles.

I don't look up. Slink might be an evil cat, but he's still right. Oggie, Kaz, Sabrina . . . It's over for all of them.

And it's all my fault. I'm like a train off the tracks, flattening everything in my path.

"Sorry," I whisper again. My brain is blank except for that word. It loops round and round and round. *Sorrysorrysorrysorry.*

"This can't be it," Kaz murmurs. I hear him pacing in his cage, his feathers ruffling uneasily. "We made it through a limo ride! Past a doorman! Away from a huge dog and a baseball bat! Through a killer pipe! And after everything, *this* is where we give up? This terrible, tiny cage?" I can hear him ramming his beak angrily against the bars, but still I don't look up.

I'm stuck on something he said. This *is where we give up?*

Suddenly I see Oggie so clearly: scurrying across the subway platform, his tiny tail whipping as he darts through throngs of feet, shouting, *Never give up! Just like Raffie!*

Those words fizz through my brain. They drown out the *sorry*s. They fill up the blankness.

Never give up!

Just like Raffie!

This *is where we give up?*

I jump to my paws. "No," I blurt out.

Across the room, Jimmy gives a start. "That's one squeaky rat," he murmurs, before returning to his sandwich.

"No, what?" Kaz asks.

"We're not giving up," I say.

Kaz pauses. "We're not?"

"Raffie the Unstoppable wouldn't give up, would he?"
I ask.

Kaz is silent for a moment. I hear his beak slamming
against the bars of his cage, again and again. "From
what I know of him, Raffie the Unstoppable would never
give up," he says finally.

"Exactly." I pace in my cage, thinking. "We need a plan."

Kaz snaps his beak thoughtfully. "No. What we need
is one of your stories."

"Uh, I hate to break up this little fantasy party," Rory snaps. "But what we need is a miracle, not some *story*."

I keep pacing. It was Raffie the Unstoppable who first gave Oggie the courage to forage on his own. It was Raffie the Unstoppable who kept Oggie from being scared of bedtime. It was Raffie the Unstoppable who convinced Oggie to make that ill-fated run for the slice of pizza. My stories are a lot of things, but they're never just stories.

Ever since I met Kaz, I've been trying to convince him that words matter. But maybe he's had it right all along. It's not just my words that have power; it's my stories, too. "Kaz is right," I say slowly. "A story can change your life."

"Unless it can *save* my life, then I don't care," Rory grunts.

"Maybe it can." I pace faster. My eyes fall on the key next to Jimmy. "What does that unlock?" I ask.

"Our cages." Slink lets out a low laugh that sets my fur on edge. "But unless your story is magic, there's no way you're getting it."

"Sorry, kid, but 'fraid he's right." Pierre sighs. "Bigger animals than you have tried and failed."

"Don't give him a hard time, y'all," Sabrina scolds. "Can't you see he's as nervous as a long-tailed cat in a room full of rocking chairs?"

At another time, I would have stored a great phrase

like that away for later. But my brain is too busy churning.

"In the Roadway, we don't get nervous," Truella says. "We fight back."

"Well, we're not in the Roadway, Truella," Slink growls. "If we were, I would have eaten you a long time ago."

I ignore them both. My eyes are locked on Jimmy's keys. "What would Raffie the Unstoppable do?" I whisper.

"Yeah," Kaz says. "WWRTUD?"

I squeeze my eyes shut. I imagine myself in my shoe box with Oggie curled up next to me. "What happens next?" Oggie would ask excitedly. "What does Raffie the Unstoppable do now?" And suddenly it's like I can see the story in my mind: just a tiny seed at first, then growing and growing until it's as big as a jungle, wild and alive.

My eyes fly open. "I know exactly what we have to do."

CHAPTER

Pull a Rabbit out of a Hat

I look at Jimmy. He's busy eating his sandwich. His soda
is still half-full.

"Kaz, do you still have that magic bean?" I ask.

"You mean the sleeping pill?" I hear Kaz shake out
his feathers. "Sure, got it right here."

"Good. Then here's what we're going to do." I quickly
explain my idea to the room.

"Now that's how a rat does it," Truella brags.

Over at the table, Jimmy picks up his soda. "It's time!"
I shout. "Commence distraction!"

On the other side of the room, the animals all start
making noise at once. Slink meows and Sabrina squeals
and Pierre growls and Rory hisses and Truella squeaks.

Jimmy's soda freezes halfway to his lips. He looks over
at the animals in alarm. "Wha— What's happening?" he
stammers.

"Now, Kaz!" I say.

I hear Kaz adjusting his position in his cage. He only has one chance to get this right.

There's a grunt, and then the little white pill is winging through the air. "Come on," Kaz whispers. The pill shoots across the room—and lands in Jimmy's soda with a tiny splash. "Score!" Kaz cheers.

That's the signal. All at once, the animals fall silent. Sabrina contentedly licks her paws. Pierre closes his eyes. Rory paws lazily at the bars of his cage. Jimmy shakes his head. "Either I'm going crazy, or it's time for a new job," he mutters. He lifts his soda to his lips and takes a big drink. "For a second there, I could swear the animals knew what was coming." He takes a bite of sandwich, then guzzles down the rest of his soda. "Like they knew exactly what I was about to do . . ." He shakes his head. "Ridiculous. Animals are not that smart. And they definitely do not understand English. And of course . . ." His voice trails off. His eyes flutter. "I feel a little—"

He slumps forward in his chair. His head lands on the table. Within seconds, he's snoring.

I stare at the key. It's lying on the corner of the table, next to Jimmy's head. There's only one cage close to it. It belongs to Truella the rat. "Can you do this, Truella?"

She flexes her patchy tail. I notice that its whole tip is gone—sliced right off. "I've survived a whole meal of rat poison before. This is nothing." Truella slides her tail through the bars of her cage. I hold my breath as her tail stretches out . . . and reaches the table . . . and stops just short of the key.

Truella wiggles her tail. She waggles her tail. It still doesn't touch the key. "I can't reach," she cries.

My breath comes out in a horrified rush.

Kaz bangs his head against his cage. "It's over. It's all over."

"Not so fast." I look at Rory. His cage is on top of Truella's. "If you could pull her cage forward, Rory, just a little . . ." I say.

"*Move* her cage?" Rory scoffs. "Never going to happen."

"Please," I beg. I lock eyes with the raccoon. For the first time, I notice how sad he looks. "This is our only chance. Don't you have a family you want to get home to?"

"Rosa," Rory whispers. He looks away. "She probably doesn't even remember me anymore."

"Family never forgets." I look around the room. Sabrina is swishing her tail. Pierre is pawing at his cage. Even Slink's tail is drooping. They all look exactly how I feel.

"Please, Rory," Sabrina begs. "I came all the way to New York City to find my daughter. And then I ended up in here instead. If we get out . . ." She trails off, too choked up to finish.

"If we get out, I could find my wife," Pierre says softly.

"I could lick my sister again," Slink adds.

"I could get back home to the Roadway," Truella sighs.

"I could finally make it to Central Park," Kaz joins in.

"Okay, okay," Rory grumbles. "I'll see what I can do. Just give me some peace and quiet already."

Rory's cage, like all of ours, is made completely out of steel bars. He extends his claws through the bottom and latches on to Truella's cage. "Here we go," he mutters. He hurls himself forward, still clutching Truella's cage with his claws. His head slams against the bars. Nothing happens.

"Try again," I say.

"Sure, just let the raccoon beat himself up," he snips. But he throws himself forward once again. His head bounces off the bars. Truella's cage groans, but it doesn't budge.

"One more time, sugar pie," Sabrina says.

With a grumble, Rory launches himself forward. Truella's cage rattles. It wobbles. It inches forward the slightest bit.

"Well, bless his heart," Sabrina gasps. "He actually did it!"

Truella reaches out her tail. This time, it hooks on to the key. She yanks it up. "I told you I could do it," she says smugly.

"Yeah," Rory grumbles. "It was all you."

"Now for the tricky part." Truella wraps her tail tightly around the key, then reaches for the lock.

"A little to the left," I call out as she feels around for the lock. "A little more . . ."

Click.

The key slides into the lock. The door springs open.

Truella scampers out of her cage. Her tail whips in happy circles as she scurries through the room. "I haven't stretched my legs in months!"

"Aren't you forgetting something?" Rory snaps. "Like maybe the raccoon who saved the day?"

"Oh. Right." Truella scurries back to her cage and takes the key in her teeth. She unlocks Rory's cage, then Pierre's, Sabrina's, and Slink's.

Slink arches his back, making me tense. "Now that's better," he says.

Sabrina leaps on top of the table. "I've been wanting to do this forever." She lifts her tail. A yellow spray hits the sleeping Jimmy right in the head. The room is suddenly filled with a very strong smell. "Ahhh," Sabrina breathes. "Just as good as I imagined."

"Disgusting, Sabrina!" Pierre groans.

"You couldn't have waited until the rest of us got out of here?" Rory grumbles.

I take a big whiff. "What's the big deal?" I ask. "It smells fine."

Pierre shakes his head. "Rats," he says.

Truella frees Kaz next. Finally, she reaches my cage. She slides the key into the lock, and the door opens. I scurry down—and bump right into Slink. His tail flicks as his eyes run along my body. I swear I can see a drop of drool forming in the corner of his mouth. I let my snout curl back, revealing my fangs.

"Relax," Slink growls. "You saved my life. I won't eat you. This time." Still, my heart is pounding a little as I back away toward Kaz. He, at least, looks completely unbothered as he flaps his wings around. "If I never see a small space again, that will be too soon," he declares.

"This time, I agree," I say. "Now we just have to figure out a new way to get to Central Park West."

Sabrina jumps off the table and trots over to us. The smell of spray gets stronger. "Did you say Central Park, honey?"

I nod. "We have to get to my little brother."

"Well, aren't you in luck? Central Park is where I was caught. From what I remember, it's just down the road."

CHAPTER 30

Like a Moth to a Flame

There's a window in the back of the room. "That's our way out of this prison," Rory growls.

I scurry up to the windowsill and twist open the lock with my paws. The other animals all gather at the bottom of the window. "On three," Kaz says.

Over at the table, Jimmy stirs. "How about on two?" I suggest.

"One," Kaz says. "Two!" Everyone pushes at once until the window flies open. Warm air rushes in. It smells like concrete and leaves. "I'm out of here," Kaz says. He spreads his wings and flies crookedly through the window. I scurry out after him. The street is crowded, humans everywhere. I dash behind a plant, out of sight. The sidewalk is hot on my paws and the morning sun warms my back, reminding me that I've lost one more day in my search for Oggie. I flatten myself against the plant, careful to stay out of sight. I can't get caught again. I don't want to lose any more time.

As the other animals file out through the window, an all-too-familiar buzz runs through the crowd.

"Do you see—?"

"What the—?"

"Is that—?"

"Oh my—"

Humans stop short, bumping into one another. Mouths open. Fingers point. Phones flash. "Is this some kind of zoo flash mob?" someone squeals.

"We better disperse," I hear Pierre say with a yawn. A phone flashes in his face. "And quick." He lumbers over to where I'm hiding and puts an old, whitened paw on my back. "Thanks for masterminding this, kid." He slips behind a building and is gone.

With a grunt goodbye, Rory leaves too, with Slink close behind. I look around for Kaz and Sabrina, but I don't see them anywhere. Instead, I spot Truella. She skulks over to hide with me behind the plant.

"I have a proposal for you." Her snout curls up as she talks, and I'm treated to a front-row view of her incisors. They're long and yellowed and the kind of razor sharp that only comes with constant use. "You should come with me."

"To the Roadway?" I balk. Even the word tastes gross in my mouth, like the time I thought I was sinking my incisors into an old, discarded apple only to find out it was made of waxy plastic. "Why would I do that?"

Truella peers out at the crowd of humans still gathered on the sidewalk. "Down in the Roadway, there are no humans. There's only shadows and survival. I can teach you, Raffie. Come to the darkness with me. I can show you what it means to truly be a rat."

I think of my dad, drilling the third rule of rathood into us. *Never set paw in the Roadway.* "I don't want darkness," I say quietly. "I just want my family."

Truella snaps her snout in disapproval. "One day, you're going to realize your mistake. I did. I came aboveground to forage one time and look what happened to me. When you come to your senses, climb through the closest sewer. Go down, down, down, until there's no more sunlight and no more street light and no more fresh air. When you've reached total darkness, when all you can smell is sewage, you'll know you're in the right place. Follow the water downtown until you reach me. Remember: in the Roadway, water always streams toward Brooklyn." Truella sidles closer, until we're snout to snout. I can't help but stare at an old gash under her eye.

"I won't change my mind," I say shakily.

Truella lets out a shrill laugh. "Eventually, we all learn the truth, Raffie. A rat is a rat is a rat. You can't change who you are." She gives me a parting flash of her incisors. Then she dashes to the nearest sewer and disappears through a hole.

She's only been gone a few seconds when Kaz flaps over, followed by Sabrina. "Sorry," Kaz pants. "We got stuck hiding in a bush until the crowd split up."

"Kaz here was a real sugar pie and helped hide me from sight," Sabrina says. "A pigeon in a crowd is one thing, but a skunk . . ." Sabrina's tail bristles. "I refuse to go back to that prison, not after you two freed us."

"Ew!" A human voice floats over to us. "Is that a *skunk* over there?"

Sabrina sighs. "That's my cue."

"Wait," I say quickly. "We need directions."

"I see it," Kaz says suddenly. "I see the park!"

I look up. Kaz is flapping above us, a distant look in his eyes.

"He's right," Sabrina says. "That's Central Park right across the street."

"This must be the east side of the park," Kaz says. "To get to Central Park West, we'll have to . . ." He cocks his head and closes his eyes. "Yes. We'll have to cross the park."

I suck in a breath. We're so close to Oggie. Sabrina pats my back with her tail. "Take care of yourself," she says. "I sure do hope you find that brother of yours." She gives me a quick lick on my snout, then turns tail and swishes down an alleyway.

I look back up at Kaz. He's flapping in the air, inching closer to the park. "Got to get there . . ." he murmurs. He starts flying crookedly across the street.

"Hey, wait for me!" I dart from plant to tree to avoid being seen. There's a look in Kaz's eyes I've never seen before. It's like he's only half here with me. He flies ahead and I have to sprint to keep up with him. I dive behind a tree, barely missing collision with a bicycle. "What's gotten into you, Kaz? You're going to get me killed!"

"Sorry," Kaz says absently. He turns back and flies in a lopsided circle above me. "My brain compass is going all kinds of crazy. It's like there are all these arrows in front of me, and they're huge and bright and flashing, and they're pointing me to exactly where I've got to be."

"To Oggie?" I ask excitedly.

Kaz doesn't answer. I look up. He's still circling above, but his eyes are locked somewhere far in the distance. "Kaz?" I say.

Finally, Kaz looks down. "I'm sorry, Raffie, but I can't keep my wings down any longer. There's something tugging at me, deep inside. I have to fly . . . I have to . . ." He spreads his wings and soars away.

"Kaz!" I shout after him.

Kaz doesn't stop. He doesn't even turn around. He flies through a thick line of trees and is gone.

WILD GOOSE CHASE: SEVERAL SPECIES ESCAPE ANIMAL CONTROL ON MANHATTAN'S UPPER EAST SIDE

EARLIER TODAY, crowds of Upper East Siders stopped in their tracks as an incredible sight met their eyes: a group of animals, ranging from a tiny rat to a large possum, climbed out of a building window and onto a city street.

The window they exited through belonged to Manhattan's Animal Control. It is still unclear how the animals managed to both escape their locked cages and open the window in order to engineer this showstopping endeavor. Only one thing is clear: it all happened in a New York minute.

"I thought it was some kind of street performance," said Marvin White, a longtime resident of the neighborhood.

"It's got to be a protest," said Summer Mills, a local student. "Stop the oppression of circus animals!"

"Ew, there was a skunk and a rat," said Sophie Walker, an employee at Dollhouse Wares, a nearby store. "All I have to say is, they better stay away from my merchandise!"

For better or worse, many are claiming the incident to be a publicity stunt staged by disgruntled employees. Mary Stowe, head of the location, remains tight-lipped on the subject as investigations continue, but she did release the following statement: "I want to assure New Yorkers that none of these animals pose a threat."

The escaped animals include a skunk, a possum, a raccoon, a rat, and a cat, along with the pigeon and rat who recently made a splash after New York One's morning show featured a photo of them falling off a city tour bus.

As of publication, none of the escaped animals have been recovered. No one knows where they've gone, but at least one thing is certain: if they can make it here, they can make it anywhere.

CHAPTER

31

Like a Pig in Slop

ait for me!" I yell after Kaz. I scurry after him, but a group of humans blocks my way. They're crowded on the sidewalk, wearing backpacks and pointing cameras at the park. I'm about to dash around them when something catches my eye. A woman is wearing a shirt with familiar letters on it. *I ♥ NY.*

"Just like Oggie's sticker," I gasp. Suddenly my fur prickles. I look up, and my eyes meet the woman's. Instantly, her shoulders tense. Her jaw unhinges. "Rat!" she shrieks.

I dash over to a bush. My heart is beating wildly as I disappear underneath it. I crouch low, careful to stay hidden. I think of Oggie and the *I ♥ NY* sticker on his ear. I'm so close. I just need to catch up to Kaz, and then he'll help me get the rest of the way.

I crawl through the bush and peek out the other side.

"Central Park," I murmur. I've never seen so much green in my life. Everywhere I look, there are trees and grass and flowers and leaves. The smells swirl together, disgustingly sweet.

I try not to gag as I scurry into the park and scan the sky. A line of buildings rises in the distance, but here in the park, the sky is wide and blue and empty. It should be easy to spot a striped-winged pigeon flying crookedly above. I spin in a circle. But no matter where I look, I see nothing but blue.

Kaz is gone.

No. I refuse to believe it. He has to be here somewhere. He wouldn't just leave me.

"Kaz?" I call out. "Where did you go?" My eyes dart frantically back and forth, studying the sky. It's unusually empty, not a single bird flying above. "KAZ!" I shout again. "Come back!"

"Pssst. Little guy." A voice drifts over to me.

I look across the field. The fattest rat I've ever seen is squatting under a bush. His belly is so full that it sweeps the ground. "If you don't want to become falcon meat, I'd suggest you lower your voice and take cover."

"Falcon?" I repeat.

"Yeah." The rat sits back on his haunches and adjusts his huge belly. "There's a falcon stalking the park. And word has it he's hungry."

"Oh no," I whisper. I picture Kaz's stubby wing

carrying him crookedly through the park. A falcon already hurt him once. I don't want to imagine a second run-in.

The rat lifts a branch. "You should probably get under here to hide. If I know falcons, this one will be coming our way soon." I scan the sky once more for Kaz. It's

still empty. "Hurry it up," the rat says. "Unless you want to be falcon dinner."

I scurry across the field and under the bush. "Whoa," I breathe. There's a wide hole dug underneath it, and it's filled to the brim with forages. There's half-eaten sandwiches and moldy string cheese and torn milk cartons and crushed M&M's and—my heart skips a beat—half a slice of pizza. The smell wafts over to me. Moldy cheese . . . hardened crust . . . rotten tomato sauce . . . It's perfectly aged. My stomach lets out a loud grumble.

The fat rat laughs. It makes his belly jiggle. "Life is good in the park." He waves his tail at the tower of forages. "Go ahead. Take what you want. We've got time to kill anyway."

I grab the pizza and dig in. The sauce slides down my throat, perfectly sour. For a second, I forget everything: Kaz, Oggie, the falcon. It's just me and the most delicious food in the world. I tear through it, closing my eyes as I swallow the last bite.

When I open my eyes, the rat is watching me. "Now that's how you eat a slice of pizza."

"Thanks for the snack . . ." I trail off. I don't know his name.

"Tiny," he fills in. He squeezes himself into a small chair and rubs his swollen belly. "Because I'm not."

"I'm Raffie," I tell him.

"A pleasure," Tiny says. The chair rocks back and forth under his weight. It's the strangest chair I've ever seen: made entirely out of smooth, glossy wood.

"What kind of forages did you build that from?" I ask.

"Build?" Tiny snorts. "Do I look like the kind of rat who works with my paws? No, there's a dollhouse store nearby. Occasionally a kid drops something they bought there, like this rocking chair. Or the store throws away something perfectly nice. Like this."

Tiny hoists himself out of the chair and leads me behind his stash of food to a shiny, gold table. It has a round mirror attached to it. "This is where I fix my fur in the morning. Look at that mirror; it doesn't even have a single crack. Humans can be so wasteful." He rubs his belly. "But that's what they've got us for, right?"

I don't answer. My eyes are locked on the mirror. There's a rat staring back at me. He has gray fur and big eyes and whiskers that droop with worry. He looks so small standing in front of Tiny's huge pile of forages. Small and sad and all alone. It takes me a second to realize that rat is me.

My fur bristles. I'm not *supposed* to be alone. Kaz is supposed to be here with me. But instead, he's out in the park somewhere, with a falcon on the hunt. If something happens to him . . . I drop my head, unable to look at my reflection any longer.

I can't lose both Kaz and Oggie. I just can't.

I scurry to the edge of the bush and peek out. We're in the middle of a large, green field. The street is far enough away that the cars are just a distant drone. Two humans stroll hand in hand along a path, but otherwise the park is eerily still. Not a single animal is in sight.

Tiny comes over. He looks out at the park with a sigh. "Everyone's hiding from the falcon. But he'll find a meal. He always does."

My whiskers droop even more. Tiny must notice, because he pats my back with his tail. "It's okay. We're safe under here. I've been doing this a long time. You've got nothing to worry about."

I stare out at the park, hoping desperately for a glimpse of Kaz. But I see nothing. "It's not me I'm worried about," I say quietly. "It's my friend. He's a pigeon and he's out there somewhere. He might not even know about the falcon."

Tiny gives his snout a slow shake. "That's not good news. Pigeon meat is a falcon delicacy."

I draw in a shaky breath. "I have to warn him."

As I say it, an awful noise fills the air. A loud, piercing squawk. A huge brown-and-white bird soars into view. His wings slice through the sky. "Speak of the bird," Tiny says.

Without warning, the falcon dives downward. He cuts toward the ground. Faster. Faster. "He's hunting," Tiny whispers. The falcon swoops across the grass. There's a distant squeak—then silence. The falcon returns to the sky, wings spread wide.

The pizza roils in my stomach. "Did he just . . . ?"

"Be glad it wasn't us out there," Tiny says grimly.

"But Kaz *is* out there." I squeeze my tail between my front paws. "I have to find him, Tiny. I have to warn him about the falcon."

"That would mean crossing the park." Tiny burrows into his pile of forages. When he returns, he has a deliciously moldy Fruit Roll-Up in his mouth. "That sounds exhausting. And deadly, with a falcon on the prowl." He swallows the Fruit Roll-Up in one bite. "You'd do better to just stay here. You'll never go hungry here, I can promise you that. I can even forage you a chair of your own." He plops down in his chair and rocks back and forth. "It would be nice to have some company for once."

"I can't." I shake my snout. "It's not just Kaz out there. It's my little brother, too." I tell Tiny the story of Oggie. When I finish, Tiny strokes his huge belly. "This little brother of yours . . . did he have a sticker on his ear?"

My heart squeezes so hard, I'm worried it's going to explode. "Yes," I whisper. "It said *I heart NY.*"

"Interesting." Tiny lifts a rotten peach and gnaws at it thoughtfully. He offers me a bite, but my stomach is spinning too wildly to eat.

"What's interesting?" I blurt out. "Do you know something?"

"I don't *know* anything," Tiny says. He takes another bite of peach. "But I've heard things. Rumors."

I can't breathe. "Rumors?" I choke out.

"Word has it that a boy brought a little subway rat to the local school," Tiny continues. "And the rat had a sticker on his ear."

"That's him! That has to be my brother!" I pace in a circle around Tiny's chair. I can't stand still. "Did you hear anything else?"

"Word has it that there's a video. The little rat kept trying to escape his cage, and some kid filmed the whole thing. He's being called Houdini Rat." Tiny hesitates. When he speaks again, his voice is hushed. "From what I've heard, the video has gone viral."

I gasp. I know exactly what viral means. I've heard plenty of subway platform gossip about human viruses over the years. Clearly, humans are sickened by the video of Oggie. And when humans are sickened by an animal, one thing always comes next. The E word.

I feel shaky all over. I have to get to Oggie. And I have to get to Kaz. "Tell me how to get across the park," I say.

Tiny rubs his belly with a sigh. "There are only two ways across the park for a rat. You can scurry through the fields and risk being spotted by the falcon. Or you can take the Roadway."

I think of Truella and shiver. "No way am I using the

Roadway. Besides, I couldn't help Kaz down there." I take a deep breath and straighten my whiskers. "It looks like I'm taking the fields."

"It's your life." Tiny reaches for a half-eaten lollipop. "But whatever you do, don't let the falcon spot you."

CHAPTER 32

Bird's-Eye View

Rays of sun scald my back as I scurry through the grass. The sun's higher in the sky now, and it feels like it's shining directly on me, lighting me up for the falcon to see. I duck my head lower, letting the blades of grass sweep over me. Tiny pointed me toward the west side of the park, but he warned me: it's not a short trip.

I scurry faster. The park is eerily still, no sparrows chirping or pigeons waddling or squirrels dashing up trees. It only serves to remind me: I'm all alone. A human passes on the pathway, but I know he won't notice me. The grass is long enough to camouflage me from human eyes. But a falcon won't be so easily fooled.

I steal a glance at the sky. It's empty. For now.

I take a deep sniff. The scents of grass and flowers and leaves and bark stink up the air, disgustingly sweet. I catch one pleasant whiff of dirt, and the distant perfume of car exhaust, but I don't find either of the scents I'm sniffing for: the feathery smell of a half-winged pigeon or the chilling smell of a falcon on the hunt.

I hurry around a tree and dart across a paved path. I'm galloping now, tearing through grass and dirt and sticks and pebbles. I cut through a patch of flowers. Their stench clings to me, but I don't let it slow me down. I lose track of time as I wind left and weave right, doing my best to stick to the grassy areas. Humans run and walk and bike past, but it's easy to stay hidden here.

Suddenly a familiar scent catches my attention. Feathers . . . talons . . .

A little ways up, a pigeon is flying crookedly through the air, his uneven wings spread wide. "Kaz!" I gasp. "Wait for me!"

Kaz doesn't react. He just keeps on flying.

"Kaz!" I call again.

Nothing. Kaz is completely focused on something up ahead.

I pause to grab a pebble and whip it through the air. It zooms toward Kaz and bounces off his stubby wing. Still, he doesn't react. I break back into a run, trying to catch up. I'm panting as I weave between two trees. There's a path up ahead, and behind it, the deepest, most enormous puddle I've ever seen. Kaz flies straight

toward it. His voice drifts down to me. "Must . . . get . . . there . . ."

"Must get where?" I shout. There's no response. Kaz is so focused, he doesn't even notice I'm there.

I skid to a stop in front of the massive puddle. I've never seen anything like it. Back home, puddles are shallow and muddy, perfect for bathing. This one is different. It's a rippling, glittering blue, too deep to walk through and much too wide to walk around. Kaz soars ahead, flying right over it. If I want to catch him, I'm going to have to cross this puddle.

I could try swimming, but I've never swum such a

long distance. My eyes land on an empty water bottle, abandoned on the ground. It still has its cap on. My tail curls with excitement. Back home, whenever there's a big rain, Oggie, Lulu, and I make boats out of foraged water bottles and race them along the watery subway tracks, while Mom and Dad cheer us on. My boat is always the fastest.

I roll the bottle over to the puddle and grab a small stick. Then I hop aboard and start paddling. Before long, I'm panting with the effort. Above me, Kaz keeps flying foward. He curves left, and I catch a glimpse of his face. He has on a dreamy, distant expression, as if, in his mind, he's somewhere else completely.

A noise drifts over the water. A low, angry squawk. I twist around. It's the falcon, and he's flying right toward Kaz.

Kaz doesn't notice. His gaze is still locked on something up ahead. A circle of tall, billowing trees.

I reach the other end of the puddle and leap onto dry land. "Kaz!" I hiss, as loud as I dare. The falcon doesn't hear me, but neither does Kaz. I duck down low and scurry through the grass, trying desperately to reach Kaz. In front of me, the falcon's wings slice through the air. He laughs, and the sound turns my stomach.

"Pigeon," the falcon says gleefully. "Just what I'm in the mood for." With another laugh, he soars toward Kaz.

"Hey!" The word explodes out of me before I have time to think. "Forget the pigeon! Look down here!"

The falcon pauses in midair. He looks down. The instant his gaze lands on me, every strand of my fur stands on end. In the corner of my vision, I see Kaz disappear through the circle of trees. I sag with relief. Kaz is safe.

But I'm not.

The falcon's deep, savage squawk fills the air. It rattles the ground and shakes the trees like thunder. He dives down, cutting straight toward the ground. Straight toward me.

A whimper escapes me. I have to do something. My dad's voice echoes distantly in my head. *Duck, dash, disappear.*

Nearby, an abandoned plastic bag floats on the breeze. I won't get far if I duck or dash, but maybe . . . maybe I can still disappear. I'm shaking all over as I hook the bag with my tail and pull it around me.

The falcon swoops lower. He squawks, and I cringe at the smell of his breath. It stinks of prey. I curl up inside the bag and squeeze my eyes shut. My heart pounds much too loudly. I can hear the falcon flying closer . . . closer . . .

Suddenly he pauses.

He hovers in the air, only inches above my bag. "Where did my meal go?" he snarls. He flaps in a circle, squawking furiously. He's so close that my plastic bag rustles with every flap of his wings. I don't move. I barely even breathe.

He swoops around me. "Where are you, little rat?" His wing brushes my bag and I swallow back a scream. I hear him open his beak. I hold my breath and wait for the worst.

"I can't believe I lost him." The falcon snaps his beak shut angrily. I stay frozen, still not daring to breathe. He takes one more swoop around my bag. "I'll go find something bigger to eat," he grumbles at last.

With a final squawk of fury, he flies off.

I stay curled inside the bag until the smell of falcon is long gone. Carefully, I peek out. The sky is empty. I'm still trembling as I shake off the bag. Up ahead, I spot the circle of trees where Kaz disappeared. I take a deep breath and wait for my paws to stop wobbling. I have no idea what's through those trees, but I'm about to find out.

CHAPTER

A Little Bird Told Me

I scurry between two trees—and bump into something soft and feathery. "Kaz!" I exclaim. "You don't know how happy I am to see you right now."

Kaz doesn't answer. He's standing frozen, his beak hanging slightly open. I glance around. The circle of trees has created a tent of leaves, completely sheltering this shady patch of grass from the rest of the park. Everywhere I look, I see pigeons. They flutter on tree branches and peck at the grass. They waddle through the field and soar beneath the leaves.

"Look at this place, Raffie." Kaz's voice is filled with wonder. "This is it. This is what I was looking for. I can't explain it, but I can *feel* it, deep down in my feathers."

"Where are we?" I ask.

"That's the thing." Kaz shrugs his wings. "I've got no idea. I was gonna ask you the same thing."

"Going to," I correct automatically.

For once, Kaz doesn't reply. He's too busy gaping at the scene around us. A pair of pigeons waddles through the grass nearby. "What's the plan for today?" one asks.

"Oh, the usual," the other replies. "Grass seeds. Nap. More grass seeds."

"A little bird told me there are bread crumbs over by the willow tree," the first pigeon replies.

Kaz's eyes flicker with excitement. He says something, but I don't hear it, because a movement in the sky has caught my attention. It's an older pigeon. He's flying in a lopsided way that reminds me of Kaz. I look closer. The pigeon's wings are white with black stripes, and one is smaller than the other. I gasp. The wing is a jagged stump—as if half of it has been torn right off. It's just like Kaz's.

"Look, Kaz," I exclaim.

Kaz draws in a sharp breath. We both watch as the pigeon flies toward a tree. There's something strangely graceful about the way he moves. It's crooked but smooth, as if he has reinvented the way to fly. He lowers his wings and lands on a branch. "Have you ever seen another wing like yours?" I ask Kaz.

There's no answer. I look over.

Kaz is gone.

"Not again," I groan.

I spot Kaz flying crookedly through the sky. He lands

on the branch next to the older pigeon. I hurry after him and scurry up the tree.

When I get there, Kaz and the other pigeon are staring at each other. Slowly, Kaz spreads out his stubby wing. For several long seconds, the older pigeon just looks at it. Then he spreads out his.

The wings are identical. The same snowy white feathers. The same oily black stripes. The same jagged pattern marking its stubby edge. The older pigeon makes a choking sound. "It can't be . . . but . . . I've never seen one that's not . . ." He looks up. "Kazington?" he whispers.

Kaz freezes. He's so still I don't even think he's

breathing. "I go by Kaz," he says finally. "Kazington sounds like some fancy-schmancy pigeon."

The other pigeon is trembling now. "It was my grandfather's name."

"Your . . . your . . ." Kaz opens his beak, but no more words come out.

My head spins faster than a train wheel. The same wing . . . the same name . . .

"My grandfather was born with a half wing," the pigeon says. "Just like my father was, and just like I was, and just like my son was. That's why I named my son Kazington. After the start of our half-winged line."

"Your son?" Kaz repeats. His voice is so low I can barely hear him.

"Yes. He was taken from me when he was very young," the pigeon says. "I haven't seen him in years."

"I never knew my family," Kaz whispers. "I just have one memory. Of a thick branch that forked into two—"

"—and a nest tucked into the crook of it," the pigeon finishes. He rests his stumpy wing on Kaz's back. "You're him. You're really him. My Kazington." He takes a deep breath. "Which makes me . . ."

". . . my dad," Kaz says.

CHAPTER

34

Open That Can of Worms

I don't understand," I blurt out. "If you don't remember this place, Kaz, how did we end up here? How did you know where to find your dad?"

Kaz's dad notices me for the first time. A ruffle runs through his feathers. "Who's the rat?"

"That's my friend, Raffie," Kaz says. "We traveled here together."

"I'm looking for my brother at 220 Central Park West," I explain. "And Kaz has always wanted to go to Central Park."

"Of course he has," Kaz's dad murmurs. "That's my boy."

"Yeah! Of course I have." Kaz pauses. "But . . . um . . . why, exactly?"

Kaz's dad rests a wing on his back. "I think you'll understand better if I tell you the whole story," he says.

"You see, when you were a baby, we lived here peace-fully as a family. It was the perfect home: unlimited grass seeds, an umbrella of leaves overhead to pro-tect us from predators like falcons, and a pond nearby, abundant with humans throwing bread crumbs. It was a happy place. A safe haven. Then one day, a new flock flew into the park. They saw our home and wanted it for themselves. When our flock refused to leave, they declared a turf war."

Kaz draws in a sharp breath.

"What's a turf war?" I ask.

"It's some nasty stuff," Kaz answers. "Two flocks fight—often to the death—to see who gets to call that turf their home."

Kaz's dad nods. "We were a peaceful flock. We didn't want to fight. But when they advanced, they left us with no choice. They were a vicious flock, and Kaz was so young; I didn't want him to get hurt. So I hid him inside a hollow tree trunk and made him promise he'd wait there quietly."

"A small space," Kaz says slowly.

"Very small," his dad replies. "But you were a good boy. You did just as I asked. You must have hidden in there for hours as the two flocks fought."

"Now I understand why you hate small spaces," I say.

"Yes, of course you would." Kaz's dad sighs. "What you must have heard while you hid in there . . ." He shakes his beak. "It was a close fight. Your mother was amazing," he adds wistfully. "She fought off some of the biggest pigeons that day. We were close to winning when I was attacked by three pigeons at once. I was thrown to the ground and knocked out. When I awoke, we had won—the other flock had retreated. But at what a cost! We lost half the lives in our flock, including your mother's." Kaz's dad's voice breaks. "It was a dark, dark day. But at least I'd kept you safe. Or so I thought. But when I returned to the tree, you were gone."

Kaz's dad pauses. A tremble runs through his feathers. "I knew right away what had happened. The leader of the other flock—"

"Ziller," Kaz whispers.

His dad swallows hard. "Ziller," he agrees. "He took you as revenge. You see, I am the leader of our flock. And since Ziller couldn't have our turf, he took the one thing that was more important. My son." Kaz's dad looks down. "If I'd known what would happen, if I'd known what I'd lose, I never would have fought. I would have retreated, given up our home. But never could I have guessed another pigeon could be so cruel."

"That's Ziller," Kaz says quietly.

"I'm so sorry, Kazington. Every week since you were taken, I've gone on a pilgrimage to a different part of the city, hoping against hope to find you. And every week, when I return home all alone, I hope against hope to find you waiting for me here. And now, finally, after so many years, I have."

"What about your stubby wing?" Kaz asks suddenly. "How do you fly such long distances?"

"What do you mean?" Kaz's dad gives his half wing a strong flap. "Our wings might work differently, but they still work. There's only one thing that can stop you from flying, and that's you. Believe me, I should know. I've flown hundreds of miles searching for you. I must have visited every corner of Manhattan."

"I wasn't in Manhattan," Kaz says quietly. "I was in Brooklyn. I always wanted to come into the city. Especially to Central Park. Whenever other pigeons took a pilgrimage into the city, I'd beg Ziller to let me go on one too. But Ziller always said my half-wing wasn't strong enough for that. He always told me it was a falcon who ruined my wing."

"Of course Ziller would lie." Kaz's dad's voice is tense. "He knew that if you left your turf, your homing instinct would eventually bring you to me."

"My homing instinct," Kaz repeats. "So that's what it was. That's what made me want to visit Central Park so badly. That's what took over my body as we got closer. It's what drove me to this spot, even though I didn't even know what this spot *was*." He looks at his dad in awe. "My body knew where home was, even when my brain didn't."

"You're a pigeon," Kaz's dad says proudly. "Home is always a part of you, even when you can't remember it. Home is stronger than logic, it's stronger than memories. It's in your heart."

I curl my tail in my paws as I watch Kaz and his dad embrace. I can't help but think of my own home. My dad making slop. My mom helping Lulu put on accessories. The whole family in the sorting nook, laughing as Oggie gnaws tinfoil into the shape of a train. Kaz's dad is right. Those things are bigger than memories. They're part of me. They're who I am. No matter what happens after this, nothing can change that.

I take a deep breath. "I have to go," I tell Kaz.

Kaz pulls away from his dad. When he turns to me, there's a sad look in his eyes. My heart sinks. "You're staying," I realize.

Kaz's beady eyes meet mine. "This is where I have to be now. Besides, you don't need me anymore. You can do this."

I feel like I accidentally ate a moth. My stomach flaps and flutters. "Alone?" I whisper.

"Raffie." Kaz gives me a stern look. "Who saved us from Rex's human-dad? And who got me through that terrifying pipe? And who got us out of Animal Control—?"

"Animal *what*?" Kaz's dad spits out.

"It was all you, Raffie. You helped Marigold and Rex

and Walter and Sabrina—and me. I never would have gotten here without you."

I shake my snout. "You're making it sound like I'm unstoppable."

"You bet I am," Kaz says.

I look down. In my head, I can see Oggie so clearly: getting trapped in that cage, and being carried onto that train, and then zooming away, far out of sight. If I'd been bigger, or stronger, or faster, if I'd been more of a real rat like Ace, not a mouse-sized rat, I could have *done* something. Instead, I was useless, and now Oggie is missing.

"If I were unstoppable, I could have saved Oggie," I whisper. "I was too small, and too slow, and now who knows what he's had to go through."

Kaz gives his beak an angry snap. "So you're smaller than other rats. So what? It's like my dad said: my wing is different, but it can fly just fine. The only thing getting in my way was me. You're no ordinary rat, Raffie. You're clever and creative and brave and you tell a mean story— and, most important, you're a great friend." Kaz meets my eyes. "The best friend I ever had," he adds gruffly. "Just be *you* and you'll be unstoppable."

Slowly, I look back up. I think of Rex and Sparkle and Slink the cat, and all the other terrifying challenges I've faced. I've done things I would have once thought possible only in my stories. And yet here I am. On the other side.

Oggie is so close. I might not have a pigeon's homing sense, but I have a brother's sense, and I can feel it, deep down in my bones. Suddenly I can't wait another minute to get to my brother.

"I'm doing it," I declare. "I'm going to find Oggie by myself."

"Hey, Dad," Kaz says. "Do you have that whole brain-compass thing going on?"

Kaz's dad laughs. "As the leader of this flock, I better."

"Tell him where you need to go again, Raffie," Kaz urges me.

"220 Central Park West," I say.

Kaz's dad nods his beak and tells me exactly how to get to where I need to be.

"See?" Kaz says smugly. "It's good to have a pigeon on your side." I give Kaz a nuzzle. "Don't get all sappy on me," Kaz warns. "Or you're gonna make a pigeon cry."

"Going to," Kaz's dad and I correct at the same time.

"Noooo." Kaz covers his face with his wings. "I'll never escape it!"

I give Kaz another nuzzle. "You're the best friend I've ever had, too," I tell him.

"Good," Kaz says. "Because now that I know I can learn to fly far distances just fine, there will be nothing

stopping me from taking a little pilgrimage to Brooklyn. Maybe I'll come for that Ratmas you were talking about."

"Bergen Street subway station," I tell him.

"It's in the brain compass." Kaz taps his head with his wing. "Now go. You've got a brother to find."

CHAPTER 35

Fish in Troubled Water

My directions bring me to a wide, brown building. I squint up at the letters on the door. *Central Park Day School. 220 Central Park West.*

I'm here.

I'm actually, finally here.

There's a window open next to the door. One quick scurry through it, and I'll be inside. I try to move, but my paws are suddenly rooted to the ground. What if, after everything, Oggie isn't in there? What if the humans already brought in the E word? Or what if one of Oggie's escapes finally worked? What if my little brother is now somewhere loose in the city, lost and alone? What if, after everything, I can't save him? The thought makes me all queasy, like I'm the one with the virus.

I think of what Kaz said. *Just be you and you'll be*

unstoppable. I take a deep breath. One thing's for sure: I'm not helping anyone down here.

I wrench my paws off the ground and scurry up to the window ledge. Inside, the floor is white and shiny. Lights burn brightly on the ceiling. There are no shadows to melt into here, no bushes to duck under. There will be no place to hide.

A girl runs along the floor, clutching a paper bag in her hand. She disappears around a corner. "No running in the halls, Sophia!" a woman yells. "I don't care that it's lunchtime!" She hurries after the girl, her heels click-clacking against the floor. She too turns the corner, and then there are no humans in sight. A tremble runs through me. This is my chance.

I scurry into the school. The floor is cool and slippery under my paws. Immediately, I smell something. French fries . . . burgers . . . juice . . .

I press myself against the wall and inch toward the smells. They're coming from around the corner, where the humans disappeared. I move closer. The smells are pouring out of a large, packed room. Kids crowd at tables and carry food and stand in line. Mouths chew, chew, chew, and the smells hit me, one after another: bread, jelly, burgers, tomato, carrots, chips, cookies, fries, apples. I spot a treasure chest in the corner, brimming with wrappers and crumbs. It has a spill of juice dripping down its side. It smells scrumptious, but I know what a room full of humans means for a rat, and it's never a good thing.

I dash away. At the other end of the hallway, a door hangs wide open. I peek inside. This room is smaller and free of humans. It has rows of tables and a big white board up front. On a table in the corner sits a small glass cage. The cage is filled with water. Colorful, tie-dyed plants sway inside.

My chest squeezes at the sight of the familiar tie-dye pattern. Lulu loves tie-dye almost as much as glitter. She once spent weeks foraging Gatorade bottles so she could use their dredges to tie-dye her straw-wrapper skirt. Thinking about Lulu brings the queasy feeling back. I need to get to Oggie. I need to bring him home.

I'm about to turn away when I notice a flash of orange in the glass cage. It's a goldfish! He's swimming in lazy circles around the tie-dyed plants.

"Excuse me," I call out. I rush over to the cage. "Excuse me!"

The fish pauses. He presses his nose against the front of the glass cage. "Far out," he breathes. The words send bubbles floating through his cage. "There's a rat in my classroom."

"I'm looking for another rat," I tell him. "He's smaller than me. He was taken from our subway station and brought here in a cage."

"Whoaaa." The fish swishes his fin. "I see it now. You look just like the famous rat."

"My brother," I whisper. My heart patters dangerously fast. "But his name is Oggie, not Famous. He has an *I heart NY* sticker on his—"

"Ear," the fish finishes. "You really are his brother. Groovy."

"The name's not Groovy, it's Raffie," I say impatiently. I feel shaky all over. "Do you know where my brother is? Is he still here?"

"Nice to meet you, Raffie. I'm Garcia. And yeah, I know where your brother is. Our cages were next to each other at the class pet competition. That little guy is far out."

I'm shaking harder now. My breath comes out in shallow bursts. Oggie is here. He's still here. "Where is he?" I choke out.

"He told me he was living in classroom 5B. That's at the very top of the stairwell, in the room across the hall. But you better be quick. The classrooms are empty now, but lunch will be over any minute, and then it will be a stampede out there. The halls fill up faster than my tank before cleaning day."

"Thank you!" I burst out. I turn and race toward the stairwell.

"Peace and love!" Garcia calls after me.

I scurry up the stairwell. The walls are covered in amazing works of art: bright, zigzagging lines and wild scribbles of color. I've heard talk on the subway platform of something called a museum, filled with famous artwork. This must be one of those places! I don't have time to admire it, though. The colors blur in my vision as I scurry faster and faster—

Footsteps.

My breath catches in my throat. A man is climbing up the stairs. His shoes rise and fall, large enough to crush a rat in a single step. I spin around. The stairs are bare and bright. There's no place to duck or dash, and there's no place to disappear.

The man climbs closer. "Yes, Principal Bowler, of

course I want to work late tonight," he mutters under his breath.

I scurry even faster, but the man is catching up. I look desperately around. My gaze lands on a loose spot in the stair's carpeting. I think of our carpet back home, the one my mom wove out of sweater lint. Oggie always hid under it during our games of rat and seek. It's my best shot.

I grab the loose patch of carpet in my teeth and yank with all my might. The carpet peels back. I dive under and flatten myself out. The man's footsteps draw closer. *Please don't step on me*, I beg silently.

"Yes, Principal Bowler," the man grumbles. "I would love to grade all the tests! Why thank you so much for the honor!" His footsteps grow angrier. Harder. He stomps up another step. Another.

Smash!

A shoe crashes down next to me. I yank my tail out of the way just in time. The man continues up the stairs, still muttering under his breath.

I'm panting as I wiggle out from under the carpet. That took too much time. I need to get to Oggie. I race up the rest of the stairs.

The top floor is narrow and darker. A shadow skitters across the shiny floor, and I scoot gratefully into it. I stop in front of the door across from the stairs. It's covered in pictures. They're all of kids holding different rats. There's a girl with a white rat on her shoulder. There's a boy with a brown rat on his head. There's a girl with a rat in each of her palms. Picture after picture after picture.

The door is open a crack. I poke my snout through and look inside. The room looks the same as the last one. Except instead of a fish tank, there's a small metal cage. A blue ribbon is pinned to the front of the cage, blocking my view of what's inside it. On the wall behind it are more pictures—too many to count. They show kids holding big rats and kids hugging small rats and kids playing with a whole family of rats. But there are no actual humans to be seen in the room. I slip inside. "Oggie?" I whisper. "Are you in here?"

A head pops up above the blue ribbon. It's a tiny, sleepy rat head. A tiny, sleepy rat head with an *I ♥ NY* sticker pasted to his ear.

The rat blinks sleepily. "Who's there . . . *Raffie*?" The rat springs to his paws. "RAFFIE!"

It's my brother.

CHAPTER 36

Happy as a Clam

I don't remember dashing across the room, but suddenly my snout is poking through the bars of Oggie's cage. I fight back a sob as Oggie nuzzles his snout against mine. "Oggie," I whisper. I can't stop saying his name. "Oggie Oggie Oggie."

"Raffie Raffie Raffie!" Oggie sings. "You came for me! I knew you would. I knew Raffie the Unstoppable would come!"

I rise onto my hind legs and tug at the latch with my front paws. The cage door springs open.

Oggie scampers out. "Raffie! I missed you missed you missed you!" I'm fighting so hard not to sob that I can't talk. Instead, I nuzzle Oggie all over. He smells different than he used to—like wood chips and too-clean water—but still, it's him. His big eyes. His round ears. His long, wavy tail. I nuzzle him harder. I know I'm acting

just like our mom does when one of us is sick, but I don't care. Oggie is here. Oggie is back with me. I dreamed for it and wished for it and worked for it, but deep, deep down, I'd been terrified to believe in it.

I remember suddenly what Tiny the Central Park rat said about Oggie being viral. "Do you feel ok?" I ask breathlessly. "Are you sick?"

"I feel great," Oggie says happily. He curls himself into me, so close he could be another one of my paws.

I glance back at the door. "Then we better get out of

here. Before any humans come." I nudge Oggie toward the exit, but he pauses. "What about my photos?" He points his tail at the wall of pictures.

"Who are they all?" I ask.

"They're my fans," Oggie says proudly. "I've gone viral, Raffie!"

"I heard," I say grimly. "Which is why we need to get you out of here. Now."

I nudge Oggie toward the exit again. But Oggie slips out of my grip. "At least let me take my ribbon," he begs. "There was a big competition yesterday, and I was voted best class pet!"

"There's no time," I say. There's a new sound coming from down below. It's deep and pounding. It thrums through the building, making the floors vibrate. "I think lunch is over." Even as I say it, I hear footsteps pounding up the stairs. I look at the door. If we leave that way now, we're bound to be spotted.

We need another way out. My gaze falls on the window. It's wide open, letting in a warm breeze. Outside, I spot the metal ladder thing Rex had called a fire escape.

I curl my tail in my paws. If Rex could use the fire escape to get up to Marigold, then maybe we can use it to get down to freedom. "This way," I tell Oggie. I lead him onto the ledge of the window. Outside, there's a small metal floor. A rickety ladder connects to it. It looks old and slippery. I peer down. The ladder leads all the way to the grass below.

"We're climbing *that*?" Oggie says.

Behind us, footsteps pound. Voices fill the hallway. I nod. "It's time to go home."

CHAPTER

37

Straight from the Horse's Mouth

And then I tried gnawing through the bars of the cage!" Oggie is telling me about his escape attempts as we scurry down the ladder. His paw slips and I grab the scruff of his neck in my teeth before he can fall.

"Careful, Oggie," I pant. The ground swims in my vision, far, far below. Back in the classroom, this seemed like a brilliant plan. But now, balancing on our paws high up in the air, I'm having second thoughts. We don't have thick, strong paws like Rex to steady ourselves. If Oggie slips and I don't catch him . . . I tear my eyes away from the ground.

Oggie is still chattering proudly about his escape attempts, unbothered by his near nosedive. "And when that didn't work, I gnawed a key out of a wood chip!

That's what
Raffie the Unstop-
pable would do,
right?" He rushes on
without waiting for an
answer. "The key almost worked too! But I couldn't
reach the latch from inside the cage. That was the first
time Tyler filmed me. He said my key was a work of
genius, and other people had to see what kind of rat he'd
found. A work of genius, Raffie! Can you believe that?"

"You are the best gnawer I know," I agree, but Oggie
is too busy babbling to notice.

"Tyler put my video online and called me Houdini
Rat! And guess how many humans watched it, Raffie?
One million! ONE MILLION! I'm pretty sure that's all
the humans in the world." Oggie puffs out his tiny

chest, and one of his front paws goes sliding off the ladder.

"Help!" he cries. His eyes widen as he teeters on the edge of the ladder. "I—ahh—ahh—RAFFIE!"

He slips off the ladder with a scream.

I lunge forward and grab one of Oggie's back paws in my teeth. He's dangling headfirst in mid-air. I hold tightly to his paw, but the ladder is slippery, and I feel myself sliding forward. Oggie dips even lower.

"No," I gasp. I just got my brother back. There's no way I'm losing him now.

I yank at Oggie with all my might, but I'm not strong enough to pull him up with just my teeth.

"R-raffie," Oggie stammers.

I have only one choice. I grip the ladder with my back paws. Then I lift my front paws and reach for Oggie.

I lurch forward.

My head dangles above Oggie's.

"Ahhh!" Oggie screams.

I wrap my paws around my brother and pull with every ounce of strength I have. We jerk back up to the ladder and land in a tangled heap. I'm panting so hard, I can barely speak. "You okay?" I choke out.

"I think so," Oggie squeaks. He carefully pulls himself to his paws. "That was . . . that was . . ."

My eyes dart over to the space where we were

dangling only seconds before. Wide open air—and then nothing.

"... not good," I finish for him. "Really not good." Oggie presses himself against me. He's shivering all over. "Come on," I tell him. "We need to keep going."

Oggie peers down the ladder. "It—It's too far."

I think about how I got Kaz through the pipe using a story. I give Oggie a reassuring nuzzle. "Why don't you tell me more about Houdini Rat?" I suggest. Oggie hesitates, his eyes locked on the long descent to the ground. "I really want to hear more."

"You do?" Oggie squeaks.

I nod. "It's a great story."

Oggie's snout lifts, just a little. "Well, after Tyler posted that video," he says slowly, "people left messages online for me. They called me funny. And clever. And adorable." Slowly, the tremor fades from his voice. "The next time I tried to escape, I used a string I rolled out of pizza cheese. Tyler filmed it again, and that's when the emails started." Excitement creeps back into Oggie's voice. I give him a gentle nudge, and he doesn't seem to notice as we climb down a rung. "Kids emailed me pictures of themselves with their pet rats. Tyler called it fan mail." Oggie climbs another rung, then another. "Did I mention I have fans?" he asks proudly.

We climb down several more rungs. "It almost sounds like you liked it at school," I say.

"Sometimes I did," Oggie says. "Did I tell you I was voted best class pet in the whole school? And Tyler figured out that I liked pizza, so this morning he brought me a whole entire slice!" Oggie relaxes as we make our way farther down the ladder. "I liked my friends, but I missed you so, so much."

"Friends?" I give him a doubtful look. "You mean the *humans*? You know humans and rats can't be friends, Oggie."

Oggie pauses on the ladder. I stop next to him. We're nearing the grass now, only a few more scurries to go.

"But why not?" Oggie scrunches up his snout. "They were nice to me. We had fun together!" Oggie looks down at his paws. "I'm going to miss them."

"But they're humans," I sputter.

"So? That's just because their parents are humans." Oggie shrugs his tail. "You can't hate someone because of their parents, right?"

I curl my tail and think about it. I never would have guessed I'd be best friends with a pigeon, but look at Kaz. Maybe, when it comes down to it, there are good pigeons and bad pigeons, good rats and bad rats, good humans and bad humans. Maybe the only way to tell if someone is good or bad is by getting to know them. "You're one smart little brother," I tell Oggie.

Oggie giggles. "Houdini Rat is very wise."

We scurry down the last bit of ladder. I blow out an

enormous sigh of relief when my paws hit the grass. We made it. Oggie is free.

"Hey, Raffie," Oggie says.

"Yeah, Og?"

"Nothing." Oggie giggles again. "It's just so fun having someone understand me again! No one in that class understood my squeaks. I did learn a lot, though," Oggie adds as I lead him toward the closest bush. "Like something called grammar! Did you know there are three different *there*s?"

"Of course I know that," I sniff. We slip under the bush. It's cool and shadowy under there. "Words are very important for stories."

Oggie nuzzles me. "I miss your stories. And I miss Mom's slop. And I miss Dad's lessons. And I even miss Lulu's passion for fashion."

"We're going to get back to them," I promise. "And believe me: I've got plenty of new stories to tell you on the way." I peek out from under the bush. Green grass sways in the breeze. Beyond it, people hurry along the sidewalk. Buildings tower over them—Manhattan-sized buildings. We're still far from home. "But first, we're going to need a plan."

Oggie pokes his head out next to mine. "Which way is home?"

I nod toward downtown. Thanks to Kaz's dad, I know the answer. "We have a long way to go, though."

Oggie leans against me. I feel a tremble run through him. "How are we going to get there?"

I watch people walk down the sidewalk. I watch cars zip through the streets. A bicycle zooms past. It has a large basket in the back, stacked with the red plastic bags that hold pizza boxes. Kaz pointed one of those out to me the night we slept outside, waiting for the City Tours bus. "Pizza delivery bikes," he called them.

I cock my head. "Huh," I say slowly. "I think I have an idea."

To: TylerLovesBasketball@gcast.com
From: Colestheman@gcast.com
Subject: Please read to Houdini Rat!!!!!

Dear Houdini Rat,

I watched your video 72 times! My friend Billy said
he watched it 99 times but I don't believe him. I
brought in a picture of you for Show and Tell. Some
of the girls screamed but then I told them you are
the smartest rat in the world and they were okay.
Olivia even held your picture. For my birthday my
mom said I can get a pet rat. I'm going to teach it
to do tricks just like you! You're my hero.

Sincerely,
Cole
Cleveland, Ohio

CHAPTER 38

Raining Cats and Dogs

We worked out a system.

1. Find a pizza place.
2. Hitch a ride in the delivery bike's basket.
3. Climb out when the bike stops.
4. Repeat.
5. Repeat.
6. Repeat.

"Thank you, pizza!" Oggie cheers. We're sitting in a basket on the back of a delivery bike, on top of a red plastic bag. The delicious scent of pizza wafts out from inside the bag. This is our fourth bike ride so far. As soon as one stops going in our direction, we find another.

"I always knew pizza was a useful food," I agree. "Did I tell you it saved me from death by flying knife?"

Oggie nods. A glob of cheese wobbles on his whiskers. We'd allowed ourselves to forage one teensy, weensy pizza pie on our first ride. I'm sure no one will miss it. "And then you and Kaz escaped from the evil pizza boss!"

"And the E word," I add proudly. I spent the first three bike rides telling Oggie about all the adventures Kaz and I had while trying to find him.

Oggie lifts onto his hind legs and takes a sniff. The wind blows back his whiskers. "We're going the right way," he declares. I taught him the trick I figured out. The farther we get from the grossly sweet smell of Central Park, the closer we get to home.

Oggie lowers back down on the pizza bag. "Hey, what was that?"

I look at him. "What was what?"

"I felt something wet on my back."

I shake my snout. "I didn't feel any—"

I stop short. I feel a wet splash on my head. Then another. I look up. Big, fat clouds roll across the sky. Water splashes in my eye. "Rain," I groan.

Even as I say it, the sky darkens. The air grows cooler. It's like the whole city is hiding in a shadow. It's still the middle of the day, but it suddenly feels more like night. Oggie curls against me. "What do we do?" he asks.

I look ahead. The bike is still moving, bringing us closer to Brooklyn. "We get wet," I decide.

The rain picks up. It soaks my fur. It streams down my snout. Oggie shivers next to me. "Think what a good story this will be when it's over," I tell him. But my incisors are chattering so hard, I'm not sure he understands me.

The sky grows darker. Thunder booms so loudly, it rattles the bike. A flash of lightning streaks the sidewalk golden. I catch a glimpse of a squirrel darting toward a tree. Then the lightning is over, and the streets are dark as night.

The bike keeps moving. I huddle close to Oggie and wrap my tail around him. "We've seen rain tons of times before," I assure him. "We've seen it pour down the subway stairs. We've seen it pool on the tracks. We've heard it pound against the ceiling above our beds."

"But there are no ceilings here," Oggie sniffles.

He's right. Rain lashes against me, stinging my fur. Thunder claps so loudly I can barely hear my own thoughts. The wind picks up, howling like a dog. There's another flash of lightning, and a tree branch crashes to the ground up ahead. Water dumps from the sky in heaps.

"That's it!" I hear the deliveryman shout. He jerks the bike to the side of the road so quickly that Oggie and I go sliding forward. I claw desperately, trying to get a grip, but the red plastic bag is soaked and slippery. My claws slide right over it. The bike skids to a stop. I tumble headfirst out of the basket.

I whip through the air and land in a puddle. Oggie crashes on top of me. "You okay?" The wind is so loud, I have to shout to be heard. This isn't just rain. It's a storm.

"I'm okay," Oggie shouts back. The wind blows harder. It whips around us, screaming in our ears. A branch flies through the air. Across the street, a treasure chest tips over and slams to the ground.

My gaze falls on a nearby sewer. The wind has blown

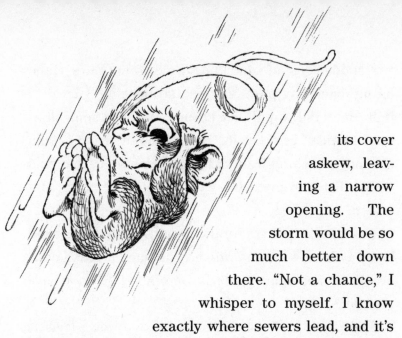

its cover askew, leaving a narrow opening. The storm would be so much better down there. "Not a chance," I whisper to myself. I know exactly where sewers lead, and it's worse than any storm. The wind blows harder, whipping my tail into my face.

"Over here!" I shout to Oggie. I dart under a nearby window ledge. Humans are everywhere, running into shops and down the street. But their heads are down so low, not a single one notices us.

"This storm came out of nowhere!" a man shouts.

"I don't have an umbrella!" a woman cries.

Oggie and I huddle together under the ledge. Water drips down my snout and off my whiskers. My incisors chatter harder. In the distance, another tree branch crashes down. "We'll just have to wait it out," I say. I use my bravest voice so Oggie won't be scared.

Oggie hides his snout in my fur. "Just tell me when it's over," he says with a shiver.

A sudden gust of wind knocks me off my paws. I land on my back, my paws sticking straight up. I have to fight the wind to pull myself up. "We need someplace safer to hide," I tell Oggie. "Away from the wind." I spin around, searching frantically for a solution. The wind whips dirt into my eyes. We need to take cover. But *where*?

I look at the sewer entrance again. Down there, we'd be away from wind and rain and humans . . . *No*. I can't break the most important rule of rathood. "Do you have any ideas, Og—"

I don't get to finish. Because next to me, Oggie is swept into the air. He swirls above me, tossing wildly in the wind.

"Oggie!" I scream. I rise onto my hind legs and grab his tail in my teeth. The wind pulls us left; it pulls us right; it throws us backward. I dig my back claws into the ground and fight against it with all my strength.

With a squeak, Oggie comes hurtling back to the ground. A sob shudders through him as he lands at my paws.

"I was wrong," I gasp. "Nothing is worse than this storm." We have to get out of this wind. No matter what rule it means breaking. "This way," I tell Oggie. We push through the wall of rain until we reach the sewer. I poke my snout into the opening and feel around with my whiskers. There's plenty of room. "In here!" I shout to Oggie.

"Where are we going?" Oggie shouts back.

I take a deep breath. I shake the water out of my eyes. "We're going down to the Roadway."

CHAPTER 39

A Drowned Rat

I wiggle through the sewer cover first. Oggie slips in after me, and together we start the climb downward. I hear Truella's voice in my head. *Go down, down, down, until there's no more sunlight and no more street light and no more fresh air.*

My stomach turns, but still we climb, down and down and down. Water runs over our backs, but there's less of it underground, and the wind disappears completely. "Are you sure this is a good idea, Raffie?" Oggie squeaks. "Dad would not like this."

I press closer to my brother. "If the wind carries you away above, I could lose you again," I say softly. "At least down here, we'll be together." I look over at Oggie. His ears are drooping and his whiskers are quivering. He looks like he's fighting back a sob. "Just think, Oggie."

I force the tremor of fear out of my own voice. "This can be a Raffie the Unstoppable story!"

Oggie's whiskers perk up. "And I get to be in it?"

"You'll be a main character," I tell him. Oggie's ears lift. His *I ♥ NY* sticker winks in the dim light.

"Oggie the Unstoppable!" Oggie cheers as we finally reach ground. I look around. We're inside a tunnel. Thin beams of light stream down from the sewer cover above, lighting up the pool of muddy brown water at our paws. A brick wall curves above and the whole place smells rotten and festering. The smell grows stronger up ahead as the tunnel twists into total darkness.

"When you've reached total darkness," I whisper, *"when all you can smell is sewage, you'll know you're in the right place."* It's what Truella told me right before I insisted I would never, ever set paw in the Roadway. At the time, the thought had sent a chill straight down my spine. But now that I'm actually here, it's nothing like I imagined. It's kind of . . . calm and quiet. "This really isn't so bad," I murmur.

Oggie winds his tail through mine. "It isn't?" he squeaks.

I inch forward into the darkness, using my whiskers to guide me. Oggie sticks close, our tails still entwined. I can hear the storm raging above, but down here there's no wind, and no rain. I take a long sniff. I don't smell anyone else down here. We've got the tunnel to ourselves. "It's kind of peaceful," I say. "It's almost like being at home. Except without all the trains and the humans."

"And no awful Ace!" Oggie jumps in.

I laugh. "Even better." I take another step and my paw makes a splash. I lower my snout and feel around with my whiskers. The water is deeper here. It gushes forward, flowing through the tunnel. It reminds me of something Truella said. *In the Roadway, water always streams toward Brooklyn.* "Oggie," I say slowly. "I think I have a plan."

I can't see Oggie very clearly, but I feel him turn toward me. "To get home?" he asks.

"Exactly. Remember that rat I told you about from Animal Control?" I say.

"Truella!" Oggie exclaims. "She sounded scary."

"She was a Roadway rat. And she told me that if you follow the water in the Roadway, it leads to Brooklyn." I pause, listening to the storm above. Wind howls, punctuated by a clap of thunder. "We're stuck down here until the storm lets up anyway. We might as well get closer to home while we wait, right?"

Oggie leans against me. "But Dad says—"

"I know," I cut in. "But think about it: when was the last time Dad was in the Roadway? It's clearly different down here now." I splash my paws in the cool, muddy water. The sound echoes through the empty tunnel. "I've seen a lot of scary places since I left home, and this is not one of them." I give Oggie's tail a comforting squeeze. "As soon as the storm stops, we can go back aboveground. And we'll already be closer to home."

I feel Oggie's whiskers twitch next to me. "Home," he says happily.

"We just have to follow the water," I say. We splash forward, moving with the current. The water leads us around a bend, to a wide metal pipe. I can't see much, but I can feel the water rushing through the pipe. I pause at its entrance. "You ready?" I ask Oggie.

Oggie nods. We climb in together. Immediately, the

water sweeps us forward. It's moving fast—faster than I realized. I reach for Oggie's tail, but before we can connect, a huge surge of water hits me. I paddle my paws, but I can't stay afloat. I sink under.

Water blurs my vision. My paws flail left and right. I can't hear anything but my own heart, pounding in my ears. My chest aches for air. I catch a glimpse of Oggie's gray fur, but then the water tosses me around again, and it's gone.

I have to get back to my brother. I paddle harder. Faster. My snout breaks through the water. I come up gasping for air. I spit out a mouthful of water. "Oggie?" I croak. "Are you okay?"

There's no answer. Oggie isn't here.

"OGGIE!" I scream. "Where are you?"

"Up here!" A tiny voice floats back to me from up ahead.

I swim harder than I ever have in my life. My paws feel heavier than bricks but I keep going. Finally Oggie comes into sight. He's just around a bend, being carried along on the current. "I can't turn around!" he yells. "The water's too strong."

"I'm coming!" I tell him. A cramp works its way up my paw, but I swim through it. Slowly, I close the space between us. I stretch out my tail. Oggie stretches out his. We hook them together. "Got you," I pant in relief.

We float together until the pipe spits us out onto

cold steel. I stretch out my paws. They wobble, tired from my battle with the water. "Are you okay?" Oggie asks. "You look like a drowned rat!" He looks proud of himself for remembering a phrase I taught him.

"It was a little more water than I expected," I say. "That's all." I cough, and a few more drops come out. "But everything's fine now." I glance around. "And look, there are train tracks here! It really is like home."

The tracks are old and rusted and covered in a thin river of water. Back home on our subway tracks, there's a constant buzz of noise. But it's dead silent here. There's no roaring or screeching of trains. There's no pounding of feet or echoing of voices. There's no vibrations as the trains rattle the tracks. I sniff. I smell only mold and rot and water and fur. A human hasn't been down here in a long, long time.

"We must be in an abandoned subway tunnel," I say. "I've heard there are lots of them in the Roadway."

Oggie looks around in wonder. "Wow," he breathes.

Behind us, I spot a grate on the ceiling. Lightning flashes above it and for a split second the tracks light up, bright as day. Then the lightning passes, and darkness returns. "The storm hasn't slowed," I murmur. "Let's keep going."

We scurry along the tracks. They're damp and slippery and I step carefully, hugging the first rail. We walk for a long time. The only sounds are our pawsteps as we splash through the water. I take a sniff every few steps, but I don't smell any other animals. Just brick and steel and must and mold and murk and—

I stop short.

A new smell wafts over. It's so delicious, it makes my stomach grumble wildly. It smells like everything good, all wrapped into one: aged pizza and fizzless soda and moldy cheese and crusty noodles and sour fruit and melty chocolate. I creep closer. Through the darkness, I can just make out the tiny round nuggets, sprinkled over the tracks.

"Yum yum yum," Oggie says. "Snack time." He reaches for a nugget.

Something clicks in my mind. Those nuggets smell really good. Amazingly good.

Too good to be true.

"NO!" I ram into Oggie, shoving him away from the nuggets. He falls onto his side and goes skidding across the tracks.

"Hey!" he says angrily as he scrambles back to his paws. "What was that?"

I lift a nugget in my paws and break it open. I gape wordlessly down at it. I was right. If Oggie had gotten even one bite . . . My paws shake unsteadily.

Oggie hurries back over to me. "What is it?"

I take a deep breath. When I finally speak, my voice shakes as badly as my legs. "Rat poison," I whisper.

Oggie collapses against me. "Rat . . . *what*?" he squeaks. I feel a shudder run through him.

"But you didn't eat it," I say. "You're okay." I say it again, just to hear it out loud. "You're okay, Oggie." I'm still shaky, though, as we skirt around the poison. I can hear Oggie's incisors chattering next to me.

"I want to go back to the street," Oggie whimpers.

"We will. As soon as the storm is over and that awful wind is gone. But think about it, Oggie." I rub his back with my tail. "Now we know what to avoid down here. So this will only get easier! Our plan still works."

"Okay . . ." Oggie says, but he doesn't sound convinced.

"Guess what," I say, trying to distract him. "I learned some new phrases while I was looking for you. Like 'every dog has its day.' Isn't that a good one?"

Oggie nods, but his incisors are still chattering. "Don't forget," I add. "When all this is over, we'll have the best story ever to tell." This time, Oggie's ears cock with interest. I keep going. "Mom, Dad, and Lulu aren't going to believe it when they hear how brave you were. I bet Mom will make your favorite slop. And I bet we get out of sorting duty for weeks! And Lulu will probably make you a hundred new accessories . . ."

I pause. Next to me, Oggie has slowed to a stop. "What are you doing?" I ask.

"I thought I heard something," Oggie says.

"Of course you did. I was talking about home."

"No." I can hear Oggie's whiskers flickering nervously. "Something else."

I cock my ears. At first I hear nothing. I'm just about to assure Oggie when I catch it. A slight scuffling. I stiffen. "Where did that come from . . . ?"

I trail off. Up ahead, a pair of eyes flash red in the darkness.

"Hurry," I whisper to Oggie. We turn around and scurry down the tracks, back to where we came from.

We don't make it far before a noise rings out ahead of us. The shrill sound of claws against steel. I stumble to a stop. Oggie bumps into me from behind. In front of us more eyes appear, glowing in the darkness. I can barely breathe as I spin in a circle. I see more and more eyes. They glow on every side.

We're surrounded.

CHAPTER 40

Ratted Out

Oggie quivers against me. I try to tell him it's going to be okay, but all that comes out is a squeak. Several animals step into view. They're so dirty, it takes me a second to realize they're rats. Their fur is caked in mud and slop and blood; some parts are tangled and matted, other parts rubbed bare.

"Who dares set paw in our den?" one of them says. His voice is raspy, barely a whisper.

"Come take a look, King," another one growls.

Slowly, a group of six rats steps into view. They move in a tightly knit circle, and I gasp when I see why. Their tails are mangled together, knotted and twisted until you can't tell where one begins and the other ends. "A rat king," I whisper.

"That's right." The six heads of the rat king talk as one. They move together too, their claws scraping against the steel tracks. The noise sets my bones on edge. Next to me, Oggie trembles.

The linked rats stop in front of us. They smell of rot and blood and something half-dead. Drool runs down their matted, torn snouts. I search my mind for a solution—an escape—but the smell is clogging my brain. It smells worse than flowers, worse than soap.

"I'm scared," Oggie whimpers. He buries his snout in my fur.

"Please," I croak. My voice quakes. "Let us pass. We need to get home."

The rats throw back their snouts. Their laughter is rough and grating. It hurts to listen to it. "Once you enter our den, you never leave it," they say in unison.

The other rats join the king until we're enclosed in a tight circle. "What do you think, King?" one wheezes. He has a gap where his left ear should be. "New recruits, or a fresh meal?"

"M-meal?" I stammer. My heart pounds so loudly, I'm sure they can hear it.

"They are still whole," another says grudgingly. A chunk is missing from his back. "She would want us to recruit them."

"Well, she's gone," the linked rats say. "We're in charge now, and we're hungry."

The rat king moves closer. All six snouts snap. Sharp, gleaming incisors flash in the darkness. Oggie cries out. I jump in front of him, hiding him with my body. "At least let my brother go," I beg. "Please!"

"Hello, boys."

It's a new voice, shrill and high. It's coming from the other side of the tracks.

The rat king freezes. All six snouts turn at once toward the voice. A murmur runs through them. One by one, they shake out their fur. They stand up taller. "Is that really you?" they ask in unison.

"I'm home," the voice replies.

I cock my head. I've heard that voice before.

A rat crosses the tracks. She's long and lean, with several patches of fur missing. She has a fresh gash under her ear, but otherwise she looks exactly the same. "Truella," I gasp.

Truella's eyes widen. She turns to the rat king. "What are you doing?" she demands.

The six rats all smack their snouts. "It's meal time."

"You know my rule," Truella says sharply. "Whole rats are recruited, not eaten."

"But you were gone," the rats reply.

Truella lifts onto her hind legs and bares her incisors. "Well, I'm back now, and this is my den." She fixes her glowing eyes on the rat king. "Isn't it?"

"Yes," all six rats whisper together.

"Then let me deal with them," Truella commands. She skulks over to us. "So you really did it, Raffie," she

says. "You saved your brother." She studies Oggie. "We don't usually take babies, but for the rat who saved my life . . ." She flicks her whiskers. I notice that several have recently been singed off. "I can make an exception."

"T-take?" Oggie stammers.

Truella fixes her glowing eyes on me. "I'm glad you changed your mind, Raffie. Our pack could use someone with your smarts."

"Raffie?" Oggie squeaks.

I step closer to my brother. My tail twitches nervously. "I—uh—I think there's been a misunderstanding," I say shakily.

Truella cocks her head. "Come with me," she says. She stalks down the tracks, away from her den, and lowers her voice. "So you're not here to accept my offer?"

I shake my snout. "We were just tying to get home, but then the rat king stopped us and—" My voice breaks. "We have our own pack to get back to, Truella." I meet her eyes. "Please, just let us go."

Truella pauses. She stares at me for several long seconds. "After this, we're even," she hisses. She turns and scurries back to her den. "Let these two pass," she growls loudly. "They're too small to be of use to us."

A three-pawed rat hobbles over. "Pass?" he spits out. "But we never—"

"I SAID, LET THEM PASS!" Truella yells. She gnashes her incisors at the three-pawed rat. A fresh cut sprouts up on his back. "Does anyone else want to question me?"

The den is silent.

"Then step aside," Truella demands. "NOW."

Slowly, the rats all move out of our way.

I look back at Truella. Her eyes look almost sad. I

think of what she said to me outside of Animal Control. *A rat is a rat is a rat. You can't change who you are.*

"You were wrong, you know," I tell her. "About what you said." My voice creaks with fear. Oggie trembles next to me. "You might not be able to change who you are, but you *can* choose who you want to be."

Truella's whiskers twitch. She gives me the slightest of nods. "Go," she says.

"Thank you," I whisper. Then Oggie and I bolt.

CHAPTER 41

Don't Let the Cat out of the Bag

My paws have never moved so fast. All I can think about is getting away: from that awful smell and those awful rats and that mangled knot of tails. My stomach turns, and I run harder, faster. Oggie falls behind, and I loop back and nudge him along. We don't slow down until the stench of the rat den is far, far behind us.

"Need . . . to . . . catch . . . breath . . ." Oggie pants. He collapses against me, gasping for air.

"You ok?" I wheeze. My stomach heaves in and out with each word.

Oggie nods, but his eyes are still wide with fear. When he can finally breathe again, he looks up at me. "Was that really *the* Truella?" he squeaks.

"It was." I look down at my paws. "I can't believe she saved us."

"If she hadn't . . . that rat king . . ." Oggie's voice breaks. He huddles against me. "I want to go, Raffie. Dad was right about this place." I stroke Oggie's back with my tail. I don't want to tell him I was thinking the very same thing.

I look up, searching for an exit. But it's pitch-dark in here. There are no slivers of light streaming down from an opening above. I cock an ear, but I can't hear anything aboveground. The storm could still be raging, but we're too deep in the Roadway to hear it. I swallow hard. There's no exit here. We're stuck.

"We're going to have to keep following the water, until we find an exit," I tell Oggie. I try to make my voice sound cheerful, but it comes out all crackly.

"What water?" Oggie pants.

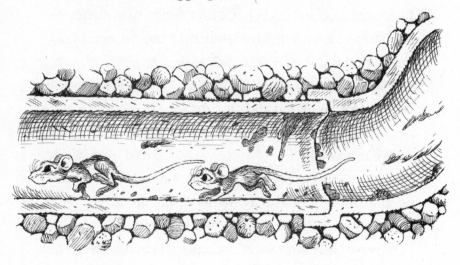

I take a few steps along the darkened tracks. My paws don't splash, and they don't splish. I quickly feel around with my whiskers. The ground is dry. Oggie's right. There's no water here. There's no way to know which direction is home.

I don't say anything as I blindly lead Oggie onward. My head is spinning so fast it hurts. "We'll just keep moving until we find more water or an exit," I say shakily. "Whatever comes first."

We feel our way through the darkness with our whiskers. I think of Mom and Dad and Lulu, back at home. What are they doing now? I've lost all track of time down here. Are they foraging? Eating slop? Are they worried about us? My breath hitches. It takes all of my energy to choke back a sob.

"Raffie, listen." Next to me, Oggie stops abruptly.

I cock my ears. In the distance, I hear a soft gurgle. "Water!" I gasp. We follow the sound to a pipe. It's dry inside but I can just make out the sound of water at the other end. Relief floods through me. "This way," I tell Oggie.

We climb into the pipe. It's smooth and cool inside. Our paws patter softly as we walk . . .

. . . and walk . . .

. . . and walk.

"Does this pipe ever end?" Oggie moans. "I need a

break." He slides down to his belly and buries his snout in his paws. "I'm tired and I'm thirsty and my paws hurt."

"Me too, but we have to keep going, Oggie." I nudge my brother back to his paws. He sags against me as we move forward. "Will you tell me a story?" he whimpers. I swallow hard. My throat is so dry that it hurts to talk, but I tell Oggie a story anyway. "Another," he begs when I finish. So I tell him another story, and then another, as we drag ourselves through the pipe.

"Look!" I croak at last. There's light up ahead. The sound of water grows stronger. I get a fresh burst of energy at the thought of something to drink. I nudge Oggie forward. "Almost there . . ."

The pipe spits us out into another abandoned subway tunnel. Grimy water flows along the tracks. I lower my head and guzzle hungrily. Next to me, Oggie does the same.

Once we've drunk our fill, I look up eagerly. "We just need to find an exit," I say breathlessly. I scan the ceiling. Nothing. I look again. There has to be an opening somewhere. "Do you see anything?" I ask Oggie.

I scan the ceiling three more times before I finally accept it. Oggie and I say it at the same time. "There's no exit."

"It's okay," I say slowly. I clear my throat. I don't want

Oggie to hear the fear creeping into my voice. "We'll find one soon. At least here there's water to follow."

We walk along the tracks, our paws splashing lightly. The walls around us are damp and crumbling. Every few minutes a piece of plaster splinters off, crashing to the ground.

"Watch out!" I yell. I shove Oggie out of the way, just before a huge chunk of plaster hits the ground.

Oggie moans, and my stomach growls with hunger, but we keep going. We dodge traps and poison. We avoid crumbling plaster. I don't know how long we've been walking when I hear something strange.

I stop short.

There it is again. The worst sound in the whole entire world.

A hiss.

"Not now," I whisper. I'm shaking harder than a napkin in a storm as I turn around.

I can just make it out in the distance. Sharp claws. Arched back. High, bristling tail. A cat is at the other end of the tunnel.

CHAPTER

42

Smell a Rat

The cat glides toward us. "I smell a rat," she hisses. "Two for the price of one." Her eyes lock on Oggie. "And look at that. One's a baby. My favorite delicacy."

Oggie backs into me. "Raffie?" he squeaks.

I bare my incisors at the cat, but she just laughs and bares hers back. They're twice as big as mine. "I'll start with the baby," she decides.

"Run," I whisper to Oggie.

Oggie scurries away. Again, the cat laughs. "Look at my paws compared to his. It doesn't matter how fast he runs, I will catch him." She strikes the air with a paw. Her claws are out. "And then I'll catch you."

My whiskers tremble. The cat's right. We don't stand a chance in a chase. I look desperately around the tunnel. I have to do something! To my right, another piece of plaster flakes off and falls onto the tracks with a splash. That's it! I race over to the wall. I dig my incisors in and start to gnaw.

The cat takes off after Oggie. I gnaw harder. A large chunk of plaster comes off in my mouth.

The cat picks up speed. "I'm starving," she hisses.

Oggie screams. He runs, but the cat runs faster. "Help!" Oggie shrieks.

I toss the piece of plaster into the air. "Tail ball!" I shout. The plaster hurtles down toward me. I stretch out my tail and bat it to Oggie. "The cat's mouth is the goal!"

The cat lunges for Oggie. Oggie

jumps away, diving for the plaster. He catches it on the tip of his tail.

"Get in my belly," the cat growls. She opens her jaws. Her teeth gleam as she goes for my brother.

"Take that!" Oggie screams. He whips the plaster at her. It zooms right into her mouth.

"OW!" the cat howls. She stumbles backward, choking in pain. The plaster is stuck in the back of her mouth.

"Score!" Oggie exclaims. I run over and he throws himself on top of me. "We did it! We won! We—"

"Need to get out of here," I finish.

The cat thrashes her head, howling wildly. "She'll get that out eventually," I say breathlessly. "We don't want to be here when she does."

I spot an air vent. It's much too small for a cat to fit through. "Perfect," I pant. We squeeze through the vent. On the other side is a row of cinder blocks.

"I can't believe we did it!" Oggie exclaims as we shimmy through the cinder blocks. "Did you see the way I caught the ball? And how I threw it right into the cat's mouth?" We emerge into another tunnel. Water runs through it, guiding our way. I take a quick glance around. There are still no exits. But at least I don't see any eyes here, or any tails. We're safe, for now. "Tail ball champions forever!" Oggie cheers.

I'm wobbly and still breathing hard, but I can't help but laugh. "We were pretty amazing," I admit. We follow the tunnel around a sharp bend. "Just wait until Lulu hears about—"

SNAP.

Something slams down on my leg. White-hot pain explodes through my body.

"Ow!" I rear into the air, but something yanks me back. Black spots flicker in my vision. I try to move again, but the pain is too much. A whimper escapes me as I look down. I'm on a flat wooden board. A metal bar is pressed tightly over my leg.

A sob shudders through me. I'm caught in a rattrap.

CHAPTER

Bull's-Eye

Pain reels through my body. It turns the world to fire. It burns inside my bones. It hurts to move. It hurts to breathe. It even hurts to twitch my whiskers.

"Raffie!" Oggie cries. "No no no no."

I look at Oggie. He swims in and out of focus. "You're going to have to pull the bar up, Oggie," I groan. "Just enough for me to get out."

"Okay," Oggie whispers. He wraps his front paws around the metal bar. With a grunt, he throws himself backward.

The bar doesn't move.

I grit my incisors against the pain. "Again," I say. "Use your teeth too."

Oggie gnaws at the bar, but nothing happens. It's too

thick. He wraps his paws even tighter and pulls with his whole body.

Nothing.

He pulls again, and again, and again. His fur rips. The metal digs into his paws. He gasps in pain, but he keeps pulling. Still the bar doesn't move. He tries again. The bar slips out of his grip, and he goes stumbling backward.

"I can't." He collapses on the ground, panting hard. "I'm too small. I can't do it." He curls up in a ball and hides his snout. Loud, heaving sobs rip through him. "I'm sorry. I'm so sorry. I'll never be unstoppable."

I look around desperately, hoping for inspiration.

But none comes. All I see are crumbling walls and rusty tracks and an old, black grate, high up in the ceiling—I gasp. An exit! Through it I spot a sliver of sky. Soft morning light streaks across it, brightening the darkness. I blink in surprise. There's no water rushing through the grate, no wind howling above. The storm is over.

If I weren't trapped, we could finally leave the Roadway.

The world spins around me. I close my eyes and fight the dizziness. Even my mind is spinning: images and dates spiraling together. Kaz and Marigold and Rex and Walter and Sabrina and Kaz's dad . . . day bleeding into night back into day . . . and now the sun is rising again outside. We must have passed a full night in the Roadway. That makes it three whole nights away from my family, and now night giving way to a third day . . . a third day . . .

A third day!

My eyes pop open. "Oggie," I say slowly. It hurts to even say a word aloud, but I talk through the pain. "Do you know what today is?"

Oggie peeks out from under his paws. "The day I failed you?" he says between sobs.

"No." My leg throbs, but I ignore it. "It's your birthday."

Oggie sits up. He's still crying, but I see the tiniest flash of excitement in his eyes. "It is?"

"And you know what I always do on your birthday?" I continue.

Oggie sniffles. "You tell me my birthday story," he whispers.

"Exactly." I think of the story I told Kaz back in the pipe behind Rex's wall. Oggie's birthday story. Slowly, a fuzzy plan takes shape in my mind. "Since we're stuck here anyway, why don't I tell you your story?"

Oggie scoots closer. He hiccups as he fixes his round, wide eyes on mine. "You have a story for me?"

"Of course I do," I tell him. "I always have a birthday story for you."

Oggie stops crying. His body relaxes. Seeing that helps my pain recede, just a little. "Once upon a subway station," I begin, "it was Raffie the Unstoppable's favorite time of day: before humans start their rush hour, but after the other rats drag their forages home behind the wall. Raffie the Unstoppable was alone on the subway platform."

Already the story is taking over, pumping through me. It makes everything else feel distant, even the pain. "Raffie the Unstoppable was enjoying a relaxing forage when he heard a noise. It was a buzzing sound, a loud one. He turned and saw them. Bees. A whole swarm."

As I talk, the tunnel disappears. The rattrap disappears. It's just me and a swarm of killer bees. The story pours out of me: how the bees attacked, how Raffie the Unstoppable tried to battle them, how there were too many, how the bees were winning. Then the voice across the tracks, tempting the bees away. It belonged to a small, lithe rat named Oggie the Brave. I explain how this young rat tricked the bees, how he risked his life for Raffie the Unstoppable.

"ZAP! ZAP! ZAP!" I finish. "One by one, the track's electric third rail zapped the bees down, until not a single buzz rang through the air. Oggie the Brave had beaten the bees and saved the life of Raffie the Unstoppable."

I blink. The tunnel comes back into focus. Oggie is leaning in close, his snout hanging open. "The end," I say.

"Oggie the Brave," Oggie breathes. "I like the sound of that. It makes me sound unstoppable. Just like Raffie!"

"Don't you see, Oggie?" My pain resurfaces, shooting from my paw all the way up to my ears. I grit my teeth against it. "You can be." I think of what Kaz said before I left the park to find Oggie on my own. The words that got me all the way here. "Just be *you* and you'll be unstoppable."

I drop my head. The pain is too much. It burns through me, making me cry out. The story took everything I had left. I squeeze my eyes shut.

I hear sounds: shuffling, scraping, gnawing. I try to open my eyes, but the pain is too great. I'm slipping under it, drowning in it. Blackness creeps in . . .

THUD!

The sound shakes me awake. Vibrations shimmer through me. I wrench my eyes open. Oggie is slamming something against the bar of my trap. Slowly, my vision sharpens. It's a brick. Oggie has gnawed it to make it resemble a hammer. He slams the hammer into the trap again and again. Fiery pain burns through me, but it's working. The bar is cracking.

"I might not be very big," Oggie pants. He slams the hammer down. "And I might not be very strong." Again the hammer comes down, rattling the trap. "But it's like you always tell me: I'm a very, very good gnawer."

SLAM! The hammer collides with the bar.

THUD! The metal bends under the pressure.

CRACK! The bar splinters apart.

My paw comes free.

"You did it!" I limp out of the trap. Oggie wraps his paws around me. He's panting and heaving, but he's never looked so happy in his life. "Oggie the Brave!" I say.

Oggie presses his snout to mine. His whiskers tickle my fur. "Just like Raffie."

CHAPTER

Till the Cows Come Home

Oggie scurries up to the grate in the ceiling. It takes me longer. I lurch along slowly, dragging my injured leg behind me. "Ow," I mutter with each step. "Ow. Ow. Ow." Finally, I reach Oggie. One by one, we squeeze through the grate.

We're aboveground, on a street. The sky is streaked with colors, and the roads are mostly empty. It's morning, but just barely. I blink in the pale light. I see a row of short, squat buildings. I see a single human, biking down the street. I see—

I blink again.

That can't be right. I rub my paws over my eyes. After the blackness of the Roadway, the sunlight is playing tricks on my vision.

"What do we do now?" Oggie asks. I ignore him and limp closer.

A square of dirt on the edge of the sidewalk . . . A thin tree sprouting out of it . . . A tiny wooden fence, with a small sign hanging on it . . . I slide down to my belly in front of the sign. Lulu could have read it in one second flat, but it takes me a minute to spell it out.

Florence's Fairy Garden.

I peek through the fence. It's all there. Two tiny stools. A little bridge. A rock pathway leading to a tiny door at the foot of the tree. "This is it," I gasp.

Oggie scampers up behind me. "This is what?"

"The last time Dad took me out for my sidewalk survival lessons, we had one close encounter. A man was taking a puppy on a middle-of-the-night walk. They got

so close I could smell the kibble on the dog's breath. Dad told me to remember the three Ds: duck, dash, and disappear.'"

Oggie stares at me blankly.

"This is it, Oggie," I explain. "This is where we disappeared! Florence's Fairy Garden. Dad joked that the fairies were 'just our size.' We sat on those stools!" I get more excited with each word. "We climbed that bridge! We tried to open that door—it doesn't really open, by the way. We were *right here*. Which means . . ."

Oggie's eyes meet mine. They're extra wide. His whiskers quiver hopefully.

"We're close to home," I say. "We're really, really close."

I drag myself back to my paws and balance on three legs. I turn in a slow, wobbly circle. "Yes," I murmur. "There's the store that Dad said Lulu loves, the one with all the human accessories. And there's the bush that's filled with bees—that's where I got the idea for your birthday story, Oggie. And there's the pizza place that smelled so good . . ."

I hobble down the empty sidewalk over to the pizza place. The smells pouring out of it are so scrumptious that Oggie squeaks with delight. I sniff eagerly. It's not just any pizza. It's *our* pizza. The one Pizza Girl brings to the subway every afternoon. The one she throws in the treasure chest. The pizza that started this all.

"When I went out with Dad, I begged him to stop here. But he said no, a rat who listens to his stomach is a rat who doesn't make it home. Then he dragged me down this sidewalk . . ." I limp my way slowly along the sidewalk. Oggie runs in circles around me to keep my pace. ". . . Then down this block." I pant loudly. It's exhausting to walk on three legs, but I keep going. "And around this corner . . ."

I stop short. Up ahead, a stairwell rises up to meet the sidewalk. A sign hangs on its railing. I can't read it from here, but I know exactly what it says. *Subway.* "Our station," I whisper.

"We're here!" Oggie squeals. "We're really, really—uh-oh."

I hear the human footsteps a beat after Oggie. They're making their way down the sidewalk. Straight toward us.

Oggie shoves me behind a tree. I land in a heap, my hurt paw crumpled beneath me. "Ow," I groan.

Oggie throws himself on top of me. "Oggie the Brave to the rescue!" he says.

"Thanks," I moan. Soon the footsteps are right next to the tree, then past it. I wait a minute before peeking out. The street is empty now. "Let's try that again," I say.

Oggie sticks close to me as I limp down the sidewalk. We pause at the top of the stairs. The familiar smell of stale subway air blasts up. Down below, a train roars into the station on the other side of the tracks. The ground rumbles beneath our paws. A few pairs of human footsteps patter softly in the distance. With a screech, the train takes off again. And then there's only silence.

My stomach flips. "Ready?" I ask.

Oggie presses close to me. "Let's go home," he says.

Side by side, we climb down the stairs.

Like Ducks to Water

We scurry around the ticket teller's booth and under the turnstiles. I slow to a stop on the platform. My chest squeezes. Everything looks exactly the same. The shiny steel tracks. The stain-splattered floor. The wad of gum mashed into the scratched wooden bench. I spot my favorite treasure chest, empty from the thief's last visit.

It's all exactly the same, but it's different, too. This place used to be the whole world to me. But the world is a much bigger place than I ever knew. It's streets and parks and sky and grass and dark, lethal tunnels. It's dogs and pigeons and squirrels and, of course, humans. It's good, it's bad, it's everything in between. "The station seems smaller," I say.

Oggie leans against me. I wobble a little under his

weight, but I don't shrug him off. "Thanks for saving me, Raffie," Oggie says quietly.

I wrap my tail around him. "Don't forget you saved me too."

The ground rumbles beneath my paws. The air changes: loosening, swirling around us. A train is nearing the station.

"Come on," I say. I'm jittery with excitement. I can't wait one more second to see my parents and Lulu.

There are six different ways to get from the subway platform to our home behind the wall: two vents, three holes, and one crack. We take the closest hole. I shuffle through a cinder block and under a pipe. I hobble around a glob of dust and take a three-legged hop over a fallen beam. A new smell wafts toward us. Spoiled . . . sour . . . scrumptious. It's my mom's potpourri. She mixes it out of gnawed-up chopsticks and rotten eggs. "Do you smell that, Oggie?"

Oggie's whiskers twitch with excitement. "Smells like home."

We climb through a gap in some insulation. It brings us to a long, narrow pipe. At the other end, I hear voices.

"It's not the same without them," my dad says sadly.

"Happy birthday, Oggie," my mom sobs.

"Wherever you are," Lulu adds.

It's them! They're in the kitchen nook. I forget all about my injured leg and race through the pipe. Oggie is right behind me. Pain shoots through me, but I don't care.

I can just make them out. They're sitting around the kitchen table. Lulu is wearing a soy-sauce dish on her head, a bag handle belted around her stomach, and a shiny red bow knotted around her tail.

A torn paper bowl sits at the center of the table. It's piled high with foraged treats. I take a sniff: fuzzy raspberries and melty candy bars and a half-eaten banana and croissant crumbs and a thick glob of yogurt and a drizzle of ice cream and a whole bunch of smashed M&Ms. It's a birthday tower for Oggie.

My mom sobs as she places the tower topper at the very tip. A moldy marshmallow, completely unnibbled. "I just hope they're safe," she chokes out. Lulu buries her snout in her paws. My dad shakes with silent sobs.

Oggie and I run faster. We're almost at the end of the pipe. "What was that fancy way you announced yourself the other day?" Oggie asks giddily.

I think back. It feels like so long ago that I picked up that new human word on the platform. But it was only a few days. I throw myself out of the pipe. I land three-legged on the rug my mom wove out of foraged Metro-Cards. "Selfie!" I announce.

Oggie jumps down after me. He tumbles to the ground and bumps into me, sending us both skidding across the rug. "Double selfie!" he shouts.

Three snouts whip in our direction at once.

"Raffie?" Lulu gasps.

"Oggie?" my dad cries.

"My boys!" my mom shrieks.

And then they're all on top of us at once, and I can't even tell who I'm hugging because we're one big Lipton family tangle of paws and tails and whiskers and fur, and nothing has ever felt more like home.

CHAPTER

A Rat's Tale

Everyone's talking at once.

"Thank the trash you're okay—"

"We were so scared—"

"I made you so many accessories while you were gone—"

"Dad's been out searching for you every day—"

"We alerted the gossip rats—"

"Where *were* you?"

Mom, Dad, and Lulu all fall silent. They stare at us expectantly.

"I went to school!" Oggie exclaims. Except his snout is buried in his birthday tower, so it sounds more like "I-wen-scooo!" He lifts his head. His fur is smeared with chocolate. "I got fans! And I learned stuff. Did you know that one plus two equals three?"

"Y-you . . . but how?" my mom stammers.

"I don't even know where to begin," I say. I limp over to my favorite chair in the living nook: a striped sock stuffed with just the right amount of dirt.

My mom gasps. "You're hurt, Raffie!"

"I had a little run-in with a trap," I admit.

My mom takes my paw in hers. I yelp as she examines it. "We need the healer," she says tightly. She hurries over to the soda can she keeps tucked behind the fort Oggie and I built out of milk cartons and tissue boxes. My dad scurries after her. The can is filled with soda tabs. They both grunt as they hoist it into the air.

Together, my parents push the can back and forth between them, faster and faster, until a loud rattling fills the room. A minute later, an old, stooped rat waddles in through a vent. He's carrying a torn, beaded purse in his teeth.

"You rattled?" he pants.

"Mr. Cashmere, I'm so glad you're here." My mom gestures to my leg. "Look at Raffie!"

"You're back," Mr. Cashmere wheezes. "Thank the trash." He crouches in front of me and pokes at my paw, making me wince. "Broken," he determines. He dumps the contents of his bag onto the ground. Straws and shoelaces and postage stamps and chewed-up gum and crumpled Band-Aids and a whole mix of metal screws.

He presses a screw to my fur, right at the spot where

my bone feels all crunchy. Then he gnaws open a straw, wraps it around my paw, and ties the whole thing in place with a bit of shoelace. "There," he pants. "Leave that splint on and it should heal up just fine." I carefully stretch out my paw. It feels better now that it's all wrapped up. "Of course, he'll need to stay off of it," Mr. Cashmere adds. "Which means all meals should be brought to him in bed."

Oggie and I exchange a look. "Cool!" I say.

"Can I break a leg?" Oggie asks.

"Absolutely not!" my parents say in unison. Before they can say anything more, the sound of pawsteps fills our home.

"What in the name of the thief is that?" my mom murmurs.

Rats. One after another. They climb through the vents and push through the insulation and scramble through the pipe. The Cashmeres and the Kelloggs, every single one of them.

"Holy cheese, they're really back," Mrs. Kellogg cries. The room fills up with questions. They fire at us from every side. Oggie clambers onto the chair with me and winds his tail around mine. In the chaos, I don't notice Ace pushing through the crowd. But suddenly he's at my side, towering over me. He's as big as ever: his huge, drooly snout, his thick, oversized paws. We stare at each other and, one by one, the other rats fall silent. "C'mon, you've got to tell us," Ace says loudly. "What happened out there, Mouse?"

It's the nickname that's followed me my entire life. The nickname I've hated with every single ounce of my being. And suddenly, for the life of me, I can't remember why.

Lulu pushes her way up next to Ace. "What *did* happen?" she asks.

I look at Oggie. Oggie looks at me. "You tell it," Oggie says.

I lounge back in the chair and rest my paws on my belly. There's nothing I like more than telling a good story. "It all started with a slice of pizza . . ."

Epilogue

Six Months Later: Ratmas

Lily Wilson sits on an empty subway station platform, staring down at the uneaten slice of pizza on her lap. "Why does my babysitter always force pizza on me?" she grumbles to herself. She pulls a Twizzler out of her pocket. "I'd much rather snack on my Halloween candy from yesterday, thank you very much."

Lily stands up and marches to the nearest trash can. She's halfway there when something catches her eye. Two thin gray tails are swishing through the trash. A baby rat emerges with a squeak. He's adorable, with big eyes and a half-eaten lollipop in his teeth. Stickers shine on each of his ears. One says *I ♥ NY* and the other *Made in Bklyn*. A second rat emerges next to him. He has a white Chinese food carton dangling from his teeth. It's overflowing with Halloween trash: crinkly candy wrappers and smushed gummy bears and melty chocolate and an uneaten Milky Way bar.

A flap of wings gives Lily a start. A pigeon swoops down and perches on the edge of the trash can. "What's a pigeon doing down in the subway?" Lily murmurs. The pigeon has a glossy green neck and white wings striped with black. He stretches them out, and Lily blinks in surprise. One of his wings is stubby, as if half of it has been torn right off.

The pigeon hoots, and both rats squeak back. *They're talking*, Lily realizes. She takes a step closer. *I wonder if they like pizza.* She takes another step. Her foot knocks into a soda can that's littering the platform. It skitters loudly ahead.

Inside the trash can, all three animals freeze. The baby rat's whiskers tremble. The other rat's tail curls. The pigeon hops in front of them both, as if blocking them with his body.

"Don't be scared," Lily says softly. "I just want to give you some pizza." She dangles the slice in front of her. "See? I didn't even take a single bite."

The pigeon hoots. Slowly, the bigger rat peeks out from behind his wings. His whiskers twitch as he sniffs the air. "I'm not going to hurt you," Lily says gently. She places the slice of pizza on the ground. "There. That's for you."

The bigger rat scurries down to the slice. He lets out a long string of squeaks as his paws sink into warm, gooey cheese. He looks up, and his eyes meet Lily's. For a second, he just stares at her. Then he bows his head, almost as if he's saying thank you.

"You're welcome," Lily says. She watches as the baby rat scurries down to join him. They both sink their teeth eagerly into the pizza. Together, they carry it across the subway platform, toward a vent in the wall.

The pigeon waddles behind them, holding the white carton of candy in his beak.

"Bye," Lily calls out. The bigger rat turns around. He lifts his tail, almost like a wave. Then, one by one, the animals disappear through the vent, taking the food with them.

Author's Acknowledgments

I've dreamed of writing a book like this ever since I was a little girl reading books like this. Chasing a dream like that is rarely something you do alone, and my path is full of people to thank.

Mom, Dad, and Lauren, thank you for believing in me from day one, for cheering me on and picking me back up, and everything in between. Nate, thank you for keeping me sane and fed and laughing, and for reminding me that I can do this, no matter how many times I need to hear it. And, of course, Florence. I always thought writing books was my one big dream—until I met you. Thank you for being my dream come true, baby girl.

To the rest of my family (Sid, Minna, Rachel, Randy, Tyler, Cole, Sean, Kellan, Popi, Jake, Sam, Daniel, Kyla, Monica, and Uncle Eric!) who have so fully supported this path and always come to every event: I'm incredibly lucky to have you all on my team. And in memory of my Aunt Michele: Florence Michele carries your name on with love.

Thank you, too, to my writing group—Julie, Alyssa, and Caroline—for helping me through this project, and so much more.

Finally, thank you to Raffie's amazing publishing team: my agent, Stephen Barbara, who believed in this book in its earliest iteration and kept at it with me until we got it right; my brilliant editor, Katherine Jacobs, who helped me to see this story in such exciting new ways; and the insanely talented illustrator, Joe Sutphin, and book designer, Elizabeth H. Clark, who brought Raffie's world to life so beautifully. This book wouldn't be what it is without all of you.

Illustrator's Acknowledgments

D rawing pictures for a living is a blessing I thank God for daily. Bookmaking doesn't come quickly or easily, so it's important to surround yourself with people who will support, uplift, and challenge you.

Thank you, Gina, my talented wife who keeps everything in life afloat, and who once asked me as I sat disappointed, "Would you still draw pictures, even if you never got published?" That question forever changed my perspective. Thankfully that was not our outcome.

Andrew Peterson, for your friendship and the friendships I gained through the Rabbit Room community. Sam Smith and Jamin Still, for being such encouraging brothers. Brannon McAllister, for friendship and tremendous support. Mom and Dad, for finding value in your little boy's doodles. Ciarra and Seth, I am tremendously proud of who you have both grown to be. Never stop believing in dreams. Tony and Judy Black, for all of your love and kindness. Matthew Johnson, your words and actions mean more to my home than you know. Ed Maxwell, for hard work and encouragement, and for always talking me down from the ledges. Katherine Jacobs, for seeing something in me that you wanted in this story.